I0535723

Under
The Shadow
Of Darkness

Book 1 of
the apprentice Series

James and Issa Cardona

Under The Shadow Of Darkness

Book 1 of the apprentice Series

ISBN-13: 978-0-9850284-8-0

Copyright © 2014 James and Issa Cardona
All rights reserved.

Any similarities to persons real or imaginary are purely coincidental.
No part of this book may be reproduced or transmitted, for profit, in any form or by any means, electronic or mechanical – including photocopying, recording, scanning or by any information storage and retrieval system without permission in writing from the authors.
Please direct your inquiries to:James.Cardona2@verizon.net

Praise for
Under The Shadow Of Darkness
Book 1 of The Apprentice Series

Finalist 2014 — Wishing Shelf Book Awards, Books For Teenagers Category

Laced with signature Cardona humor ... hard choices to be made... and a few handy life's lessons ... at the sharp end of the bloodthirsty undead hordes' teeth, which certainly keeps his motivation and the overall pace of the book at a rollicking clip. ...A most worthwhile read.
—**Marc Secchia, author of** *The Pygmy Dragon* **and** *Shapeshifter Dragons* **series**

A thoroughly entertaining read sure to please middle graders!
—**Kirsten Jany, author of** *Enter To Win*

Fun, interesting, and I really enjoyed the characters
—**Meghan, The Gal In The Blue Mask Book blog**

Light vs dark, Good vs Evil, greed, a quest, adventures, walking dead! This wonderful adventure novel will appeal to all ages.
—**Laura, Dogsmom Visits Book blog**

Also by James Cardona

Coming Soon: The Dragon's Castle : apprentice 2

Coming Soon: The Worthy Apprentice : apprentice 3

Santa Claus vs. The Aliens

Gabriella and Dr. Duggan's Secret Dimensional Transport
Machine : NuGen 1

Gabriella and The Curse of The Black Spot : NuGen 2

Gabriella and The Speed of Life: The Complete Nugen Series

map of the known world

the apprentice series ~James Cardona

Table Of Contents

1 The Home of the Master   1

2 Ghoul-kind   13

3 Ulysses or Odysseus   21

4 The Hinterlands   31

5 Ghoul Speak   47

6 Sha'ane Village   57

7 The Mayor of Sha'ane   66

8 Bite Me   79

9 And Then There Were Three   100

10 Protolith   123

11 Ghoul Attack   139

12 Alexius and His Band   151

13 Hell Hounds   171

14 Fleck   182

15 Valley of Death   194

16 The Breach   208

17 Rylithnon   222

18 Truth Shines   239

Table Of Contents

Acknowledgments   247

Coming Soon!   249

About the Authors   261

Chapter One

Home of The Master

Bel's prearranged speeches quickly escaped him so he recited the standard presentation. "Master Nes'egrinon, I am Bel. Graduate of Lasaat and your chosen apprentice. I present myself to you for service and training." He said the words nervously. On the long journey from the University of Arts and Magic he had rehearsed his words and how he would say them many times but he did not expect others to be present when his prepared announcement rolled off of his tongue. And he certainly did not expect to see Kerlith's grinning face in the shadows.

"Very well. Enter, Fifth Year student of Lasaat," the

old man replied.

Kerlith choked back a laugh and masked it by coughing. Bel tried to ignore it. They had a history but Bel wanted to make a clean break; he wanted to start over fresh.

Fingers of light highlighted old scars on one side of Nes'egrinon's face as he turned and pointed his crooked finger. "Stand there, in that corner, Fifth Year. I have guests and we are attending to business. I will speak with you shortly."

Bel, thin and lithe, not quite a boy and yet not quite a man, went quietly and watched. Nes'egrinon returned to his chair in front of the fireplace and gave his back to the other mage in the room, a stone mage much younger than Bel's new master. Bel had never seen much less heard of a mage giving another of equal stature his back. It would be considered the gravest of insults, but Nes'egrinon did it causally and apparently without malice.

Muolithnon said, "Please consider the facts, Nes'egrinon. If the situation were not so, I would not trouble you." He walked around the room to stand near the fire so that the old wizard might look up at him but his gaze did not leave the flames.

"I believe you, even though I haven't seen it myself." The gray bearded mage paused as if he was suddenly listening to a faint sound. "The wind in the trees... There is death in the air. I don't know what it is. It hides from me."

"Aye. And the stonecutters. It is well known that they speak only truth. Their words are troubling to hear. Even for such a one as you who has seen much, these are worrisome times. Something needs to be done. This is why I am here. This is why I have left my home of stone to ask for your help."

Bel had heard rumors that Nes'egrinon was odd. Standing in the corner and gazing around at the hovel, he realized that none of the stories did any justice to the old wizard or his home and its piles and piles of odd looking, dirt-covered junk stacked to the ceiling. The place was filthy too. A thin twilight shining in from the solitary window paralyzed the heavy dust hanging low in the air. The hearth was the centerpiece of the home and its flames flickered warm light on the moss-filled cracks of the stone floor; it felt much like an animal's burrow to Bel.

"Fifth Year, water." Nes'egrinon's words were hard in Bel's ears but he complied without a look or a word. He did not like being called Fifth Year and did not expect to so quickly be ordered about like a First Year. Of course he knew he was to serve his master; washing, cleaning, cooking, it was all part of the deal. He had just graduated from the University of Art and Magic, one of the most prestigious schools in all the lands, and after graduation he was selected by Nes'egrinon, the great and terrible Nes'egrinon. It made his decision so much more difficult but he did it; he took the vow of celibacy, the vow that all wizards in training must take, and he left the girl he loved and the dream of a different life behind. Shireen. Her name popped into his head, but he pushed it away. Now he would serve his master and serve him well. In exchange he would learn from one of the greatest wizards in all the lands. If he lived.

Trepidation momentarily tore at him but he quickly choked it back, trepidation at being passed over by every mage during selections, every mage except one. Sure, some students didn't get selected at all so Bel was happy when he found out he was picked but he wondered if not being chosen may have been better than being chosen by someone who everyone thought would get him killed. He had hoped that the rumors were not true and everything might turn out fine but still he lamented being chosen by Nes'egrinon, the great Nes'egrinon, who for all his legendary exploits had only ever taken two apprentices, two apprentices who it was said both died before they completed their training. Bel remembered the rumors. It was said that they died before making it out of their first year under his hand.

Kerlith smirked then returned his attention to his teacher. He seemed to thoroughly enjoy that Bel was being ordered to fetch like one of the untrained. Bel didn't flinch as he filled the cup but his mind quickly returned to that fateful night and how it had happened. His self-loathing for accepting Kerlith's challenge at the University grabbed him anew, the challenge that resulted in him being held back when his fellow students graduated in their fifth year, at least the ones that made it that far. He hated being the only Sixth Year at the University. But he was out now; everything was different; he was a wizard in training. He had to squeeze Kerlith and what he had done out of his mind.

The old wizard continued, "So you think the stonecutters only speak truth, do you? That hasn't been my experience."

Muolithnon replied, "Master Nes'egrinon, we should not argue about such things. The war is long over. We have a common problem and I would think that we could solve it." The mage stepped a bit closer to the old man and said, "Let us make this grand bargain. We will travel past the Hinterlands, past the Keep of the stonecutters. Let us see what we shall see and if the rumors are true. Let's find out if the stonecutters speak rightly or if it is just madness and drink and shadows. And the trees... let us see if what you, ah, hear is true. Yes, let's see what abomination has caused all of this. If indeed it is the unspeakable then we will send for the others to join us." Muolithnon spoke with a smile as if what he said was easy and common.

Nes'egrinon's eyes remained on the hearth. He replied, "And leave my forest unguarded?"

Bel placed a full cup of water into Nes'egrinon's aged, shaking hand.

"Your western edge has seen no challenge for decades and your eastern edge is guarded by my borders, is it not?" The mage stopped smiling and rubbed the large stone pendant hanging from his neck. "I understand your concern as I am dedicated to my charge as well. I am the mage of the eastern stone lands and I must do what I can to protect my people. That is why I implore you to come with me. Let us journey under the shadow of darkness. Let us find the source of this eternal night."

"Mmmmm. Now that's what a cup of water should taste like."

Muolithnon pursed his lips. "Master archmage? Will you join me?"

Nes'egrinon looked away from the fire and placed his piercing eyes on the mage. He was old; he remembered a time long before the magician who stood before him was even born, a time when their lands were at war, a time when many of his people died at the hands of the stonecutters. "Listen. I think your idea is stupid. I mean, on the surface it seems like the right thing to do. There are some problems over there so, 'Hey let's go investigate,' but listen to me. No one knows when they are making a mistake until after they have already made it and it blows up in their face." The old wizard paused then continued, "Well, maybe that's not entirely true. Everyone knows that poking a dragon in the eye is a mistake. Yes, I should have known better, but in general, we don't know until it's too late." The old mage turned to Bel and said, "Fifth Year, attend to their horses. Muolithnon, please, you and your apprentice are welcome to stay the night here, but I cannot join you. My place is here at the edge of the Greenlands."

Bel wanted to stay and listen to the discussion but he knew he had to see to the horses so he went outside and called mage-light into his short staff. He had never heard masters disagree openly at Lasaat. He wanted to listen so he went to the horses hurriedly so that he might return and not miss too much.

"Come horse, come." Bel said as he untied the Gidran's reins. He led the horse to the back of the hovel then filled the trough with water. Bel retrieved the pony, Kerlith's horse, and tied it next to the large brown horse and placed some feed in their bags. As he walked back towards the front of the small structure he heard an unsettled neigh. The young boy returned quickly to check the horses, knowing that he was most assuredly missing all the best parts of the conversation inside. That stone mage doesn't look like he is going to take no for an answer. Especially after traveling so far. And my new master, he sure doesn't pull any punches, does he?

He stroked the Gidran's long nose and said, "What is it, boy?" His staff light shone in the horse's face and suddenly Bel felt a shiver of fear. The horse was afraid. "It's alright, horse. You have nothing to fear. We are on the edge of the forest. No men war here. And no gypsies would dare steal you. No, not with two of the great ones inside. Ha." Bel laughed at the thought.

Suddenly a rustling at the edge of the forest caught Bel's ear. He had been here, at the mage Nes'egrinon's home, for only a short time so he was not yet accustomed to the sounds and noises of this region. He did not know what creature of the night would make such a noise. It was dark. It was night. And Bel was a boy from the city. In the far horizon he could still see the fading sun but here it was the darkest night. Bel stood silent, peering into the forest, looking for the source of the noise.

Probably squirrels, Bel thought. He remembered his forest training at Lasaat. Large animals such as deer or elk tended to be very quiet to avoid detection from predators while very small animals such as squirrels take the opposite approach, making large amounts of noise to scare off animals that would eat them.

Bel stretched forth his mind and became one with all that was living as he often practiced at the University of Arts and Magic, calling the surrounding light to him, slowly coaxing it.

"Ela, ela, ela. Ela, phos, ela" Bel called out the mage-words softly as he caused light-desire to fill his being. Small beams of life streamed in from the surrounding darkness, gathering into increasing larger pinpoints around him. Bel smiled. He asked the lights to join, to become one, to enter the top of his short wooden staff, forming a ball of soft dancing light. Then he pointed the staff toward the forest.

The horses pulled and bucked.

"Calm down. Calm down." Bel held his hand to the side of the Gidran's neck and pushed peace into it. The horse shook his head in disagreement and blew air out of its mouth across its lips. The young pony pulled and shook also but Bel was less worried about it since it was not strong enough to break its reins.

Red eyes appeared at the edge of the forest, low to the ground. Then another pair appeared, then another.

"Hello, what's this then?" Bel questioned out loud.

The horses yanked again and again and Bel knew that they were pulling too hard for him to move them back to the front. He had to calm them down first.

Bel pointed his staff straight and called out words in the mage-language. The ball of bouncing light sheltered in the curved end of his staff grew suddenly brighter then plodded out. As the flare slowly arced out of the staff and sailed across the small grassy opening and into the woods, it revealing about ten gray faces, their bodies crouching down at the edge of the woods, their crooked teeth exposed in snarls then the light quickly went out. Bel and the horses were enveloped in darkness.

The horses buckled harder and the Gidran's reins snapped. The large horse galloped away before Bel could grab at it. Gurgling noises surrounded Bel as the creatures emerged from the edge of the forest. Bel couldn't see them. He suppressed his fear and blindly tried to untie the heaving pony.

The mage-words flowed out of him quickly, "Phos. Phos. Phos," each time more desperately but the light did not come. His hands found the pony's reins, stretched hard and taut, and he tugged on them, trying to create slack so he could free the small horse. It yanked and tugged, attempting to break free, squealing and wheezing fiercely. As Bel struggled with the reins in the dark he could feel an increasing presence around him. They were surrounding him.

"Phos. Phos. Phos!" No light came. It was as if all the life had been squeezed from the world.

The pony bucked and heaved, neighing loudly, desperate to escape, yanking on the reins, trying to break them. Bel felt hands on his shoulders and arms and legs. Cold, probing hands touched his face and ran fingers in his hair. A wheezing dank breath was in his ears. They were all around him. Coldness surround Bel. He shivered hard and uncontrollably.

"Phos! Phos! Parakalo! Phos!" Far off a tiny glimmer twinkled into the space, a dim flame, less than that of a single candle, but enough, just enough to see the gray faces of the creatures mounted on the pony, crawling all over it and standing around it, placing their gray hands in it. They were people, at least they looked like people, but their skin appeared gray and dead. An earthy, moldy, repugnant smell hung in the air; Bel snorted trying to escape the rancid odor. Then one of the gray creatures opened its mouth wide revealing rows of black teeth, looked at Bel, smiled gruesomely and slowly sunk his fangs into the young pony's flesh.

Bel howled, "Ghouls!" and sent power into his staff.

"Apokrothos!" A burst of energy sent a few of the close ghoul-kind flying high in the air and off into the woods. Bel loosed the pony but before he could get control of its reins it pulled away and ran. He scampered back toward the front trying to convince himself that he actually saw what he thought he just saw. He had never seen a ghoul in person but the descriptions in the ancient histories at Lasaat were accurate enough. Ghouls! I can't believe it! As he feverishly pushed to the front more ghoul-kind reached out toward him. He plowed through a pile of ice-cold hands and arms reaching out toward him, trying to slow him down and pull him away. He repelled them and ran in the dark around the edge of the hovel, trace echoes of what he just saw burnt into his vision. He rounded the front corner, flung open the door, leapt inside, slammed the door hard behind him and pressed his back against it. Wide eyed, he returned three questioning gazes.

"There's—there's—there's ghouls! Out there! In the

forest! Ghouls. I saw them. In the forest."

Chapter Two
Ghoul-Kind

Nes'egrinon looked up at Muolithnon, puzzled. "Ghouls? Here? Is that possible?"

"Aye," Muolithnon replied somberly.

"Why didn't you tell me that ghoul-kind were about?"

"I didn't think you would believe me. I can barely believe it myself."

"Ghouls. Here." Nes'egrinon shook his head. "It is hard to believe."

Muolithnon calmly explained, "The stonecutters first reported seeing one a few months ago. We investigated, thinking it nothing more than a child's story or the rantings of those that sit too long at the inn, trying to frighten the barmaids."

"And?"

Muolithnon added, "And we found nothing. No sign of ghouls, but for one thing. Stonecutters were disappearing from the quarries. Their master's complained. Wanted us to track them, bring back their workers. We didn't think they were related. Then we found the blood."

"How much?"

"Not much. But it wasn't hard to find. The death trails were open."

"I see," Nes'egrinon said pensively.

"But Nes'egrinon, honestly, I did not expect them here. I wonder if they followed us."

"Huh."

Muolithnon stood and pulled his vest tight then addressed his apprentice, "Kerlith. Come. Let us see how your training holds up."

Kerlith grinned at Bel and rolled the stone medallion hanging from his neck with his thumb and index finger as small red flames danced around it. Bel stepped out of their path and placed questioning eyes on Nes'egrinon.

The aged mage struggled from his chair, retrieved his tall staff and hobbled to the door. "Ghouls, huh? And in my forest no less. Let's have a look see, I suppose." Stepping through the single entry to his one room shack, he turned to Bel and said, "Now you stay put. I haven't even had a chance to talk to you yet. Don't want you getting killed before I've had a chance to tell you how this is all going to go."

Bel closed the door behind them and thought about latching it but then reconsidered. He went to the lone window and peered out into the blackness as Kerlith stepped out from behind the spell of protection and walked out into the clearing.

Kerlith stood in the middle of the front yard of the hovel, Muolithnon and Nes'egrinon a few paces behind him but they could barely see each other. It was too dark.

Rustling and movement was all around Kerlith. He removed the stone from his neck and gripping it firmly in his hand, held it far above his head and cried out, "Elampo!" The ground rumbled softly as small objects pushed up out of the earth. The ground was covered with them, small jagged crystals beaming a variety of different colored lights: blues, pinks and purples. The glowing ground exposed the ghouls, more than ten of them, maybe more than twenty, and momentarily disoriented them. Then they advanced on Kerlith from all angles.

The old wizard said, "Well now look at that. Ghouls. And right here, off my front doorstep."

Muolithnon held the side of his head and Kerlith heard, "Remember your training. Don't panic."

Kerlith allowed several of the ghouls to approach. They smiled as they placed their hands on him. One of them shallowly whispered, "Blood. We need blood."

Some ghouls pushed and pulled, yanking each other out of the way, trying to be the first to taste blood. Kerlith extended his arms, his eyes clenched down tight, him mumbling words, pushing out from deep in his belly, reaching deep down within himself and pushing outward. A few ghouls touched Kerlith then immediately withdrew their burnt and blackened hands and retreated a few paces.

One cried out as his hand withered, "Why? Why do you hurt us?" He tucked the mottled appendage into the folds of his clothing.

Kerlith proclaimed, "Leave this place. Return to your home."

Many of the ghouls murmured to each other, contemplating whether they should heed the words of the single young man when they numbered so many. A group of them began walking toward the apprentice en masse. Kerlith looked back at Muolithnon who nodded then turned to Nes'egrinon and said, "Obstinate, aren't they? Shall we teach them a lesson?"

"Maybe," the wizard grunted. "You first. I'll stay here and watch for now."

The young-looking mage stepped off the front porch and as his foot struck the grass, stepping out from behind the spell of protection on the hovel, the heads of many ghouls suddenly snapped toward him. Other ghouls erupted from the surrounding woods. Then a larger one, shirtless and scarred, ripped through the pack of them and screamed, "Mage!" The cheering ghouls stampeded towards Kerlith and his master while Bel nervously stroked his short staff on the other side of the window.

Muolithnon joined his apprentice as the ghouls enveloped them. The shirtless one howled, "MAGE BLOOD!" and launched himself in the air at Muolithnon, swinging a thick tree branch, striking the wizard on the head. The wizard collapsed to the ground in a heap. The other ghouls fell upon them, mouths open, teeth glistening, ready to bite, ready for blood.

Bel knew his new master told him to stay inside but surely he would forgive him for coming to their aid. He was a graduate of the finest wizardry school in all the lands after all. He wasn't a First Year. He knew how to do some things. He could help them. Bel grabbed his staff in his hand firmly, placed his hand on the doorknob, turned it and stepped outside into the darkness.

Ghouls were trying to pull Muolithnon's fallen body away so Nes'egrinon slammed the tip of his staff into the ground, sending out a tremor, an earthquake, toppling many of the ghouls, then stepped off the front stoop and joined them. Bel shook and fell but quickly scrambled to his feet and ran to Muolithnon's collapsed frame.

Kerlith held his stone in front of him while the elder mage lifted his long staff high, both shining forth blinding light and power. The ghouls circled them crying out with increasing ferocity, "Mage blood! Give us some mage blood! Just a drop. Just a little. It is all we ask!" but they cowered from the bright mage-light.

Kerlith pushed a flash of light into his stone to get their attention then announced, "You will have no blood this evening! Mage or otherwise! Now return to your home and rest. Anapauomai. Pao. Anapauomai."

Somehow, when the young apprentice said "rest" in the mage-language the ghouls calmed. Some reluctantly turned their backs and began walking back toward the forest. Others slouched and looked down at the ground as if they were reminded of who they were and where they belonged.

Nes'egrinon suddenly noticed Bel in the fray and looked on in horror as Bel held out his staff at a pack of ghouls and hissed, "Salatario!"

The group began to hop and dance ecstatically, crying out, "Yes! Yes! Yes!"

The old mage moved quickly to Bel's side and caught him as he fell back unconscious. He laid Bel's body next to Muolithnon's then held his staff high and pushed hard. A bright light erupted from his staff and pierced the darkness. The ghouls sheltered their eyes as the gray mage exclaimed, "Pao! Be gone! Be gone before I become angry!"

The ghouls paused, looking up at the old wizard, feeling the shine of his power, then slowly, one by one, wandered back into the woods. After the last of the ghouls left, the old mage lowered his staff, allowed its light to extinguish and said, "Kerlith, come. Carry your master inside."

Kerlith bent down, threw his master's arm over his neck and dragged him into the hovel. The old mage reached down and wrapped Bel's pant legs in his hands and dragged him by his feet, Bel's head bouncing and bobbing on stones, steps, the porch edge and threshold. Then Nes'egrinon closed the door.

The gray bearded mage laid his staff on Bel's crumpled body and said, "Baru." The staff sunk into Bel's clothing and pinned him to the floor. The old wizard placed his foot upon Bel's cheek and pushed, rolling his head over. He crinkled his face and called for the poison to flow out from his body in the old language. Bel coughed lightly as a black liquid slowly leaked from his mouth. Nes'egrinon walked away mumbling, "Fool boy. Why did I take on another? Why?"

Kerlith said, "Good master? Where shall I place my teacher?"

Nes'egrinon pointed back at his bed without turning around. "There. In my bed. Lay him on my bed." The old man poured himself a cup of water from a pitcher and added a pinch of dust from a jar. He addressed Kerlith as he drank, "Is this what they teach you now in that school?" pointing at Bel's body.

"No. I don't know. I don't know why he didn't stay inside." Kerlith wiped the blood from his master's forehead then added, "I don't know why he didn't listen. I would have."

Nes'egrinon walked across the small one room structure and examined the gash on Muolithnon's head then placed his hand upon it. After a few moments he removed his hand and the wound was noticeably smaller. He said, "It will heal. It will heal." He cleared his throat and rested his weight on the bed frame, then continued, "I must rest. Leave your master there to sleep in my bed. In the morning we will discuss this further."

"And Bel? Do we leave him there?"

The old wizard slumped into his chair in front of the fire, slowly closed his eyes and exhaled. "It's as good a place as any."

Chapter Three

Ulysses or Odysseus

Bel's eyes peeled open and his vision slowly cleared. Looking around at the hovel he didn't immediately know where he was. And then it came to him. He was in Nes'egrinon home. Bel tried to stand up but couldn't move.

Seeing Kerlith sitting at the table, playing with pebbles, dancing them in the air, he called out, "Hey. A little help here?"

Kerlith looked over at him and said, "You have to wait for your master. He pinned you down."

"I can see that. I can't move."

Kerlith smiled. "You really screwed up last night. Typical. What'd you do?"

"Poison."

"Hahaha. They're dead. What'd you think that would do?"

"I don't know. I saw your master lying on the floor unconscious. There were too many of them. I just thought I should do something. I wanted to help."

Nes'egrinon bellowed from across the room, "You *wanted*? You *wanted*? Here you do not do what you *want!*"

Kerlith looked down. "Bel, I think your master is awake."

Bel tried to twist his head toward the direction of the old wizard's voice, but from his position he couldn't see him. "Master, I'm sorry. I have only been here a short while and I've already gotten you upset with me. It will not happen again."

Nes'egrinon rose from his chair, walked across the room and stood over Bel, his eyes barreling down into him. "You have yet to see me angry. Just don't do something stupid like that again." He reached down and placed his hand on his staff and said, "Eukalos," then removed the wooden stick from Bel's body.

Bel stood up dizzily, placing his hand on the door frame for support. "Master? What happened to me?"

"You did something stupid. You had no clue what you were dealing with and you threw yourself into the middle of it, waving your stick around like you were an idiot trying to save the world. All you Fifth Years are alike. Running around waving your sticks like you know something when you don't have a clue. A good way to get yourself killed. And worse yet, a good way to get me killed. Now that's something that I don't want to think about. Some idiot kid running into a fight and getting me killed. I certainly don't need that right now." The mage walked back to his chair and sat. "Of course, most people are stupid so you got that going for you. At least around here anyway. Maybe it's me. Do I attract stupid people or something?" The mage looked at the fire and continued rambling, "Anyway, Fifth Year, don't let it get you down. You didn't kill yourself and you didn't get me killed. You just did something stupid. We'll leave it at that for now."

Bel coughed up mucus, swirled his finger in his mouth and looked at the black goo mixed in with his saliva.

Nes'egrinon exhaled in frustration then said, "Apprentice? Err, what's your name? Kerlith, right? Tell the Fifth Year what you know about ghoul-kind. I'm tired of talking."

Kerlith looked at Bel and for once in his life felt sorry for him. They had competed in everything at Lasaat and he loved to see Bel fail but for once Kerlith decided to defend him. "Bel, I know they didn't teach us much about the dead at Lasaat. I learned everything I know about them quite recently. Even my master has little experience with them. We are defenders of the mountains, the land of the stonecutters. Our magic is of crystals and minerals, not ghouls and the dead." Kerlith paused and glanced at Nes'egrinon to see if he was listening but his gaze never stirred from the hearth.

He continued, "Bel, do you remember anything about the dead, any of the stories from the University?"

Bel coughed then sat down on the floor. "I remember one."

"The one about Ulysses?"

"Odysseus. I rather call him Odysseus. It was in our History of Magic class, I think."

"That's the one I was thinking of," Kerlith replied.

"I remember it going kind of like this. So, Odysseus, a great wizard, visits the underworld—I don't remember how he got there—and he sees the dead. I seem to remember them being described as ghosts? Or shadows of their former selves?" Bel said.

"That's what I thought too."

"Then Odysseus gives them blood to drink. As they drink the blood they become more substantial. More... human. They can speak to Odysseus like any human would. Since a bunch of them died in different parts of the world, including Odysseus' home town, they were able to give him information on what was going on there before they died. Some of them died recently so the information ends up being valuable." Kerlith turned in his chair. "That's about all I remember. Except one other thing."

Bel looked up at him and questioned, "What's that?"

"There was one of the dead that Odysseus spoke to who was a seer."

"Oh yeah."

"And the seer could still see in the underworld. He still had his gift of sight. Even though he was one of the dead, he could still see into the future. He just needed some blood to do it."

"Right. I remember that now. They were people, all kinds of different people, with all their human knowledge and their abilities. They were just dead."

"But they never taught us how to fight them at the University." Kerlith looked at the old mage again but he was still staring at the fire.

"How did you learn?" Bel asked.

"Much like you. We tried some things that didn't work, but luckily it was only on singles. We never tried anything on a group like last night."

"And what worked?"

Kerlith snickered. "Well, poison certainly doesn't. That only makes them stronger."

"I know that now. What else? How were you burning them?"

"Healing," Kerlith stated plainly.

"Healing?"

"The same way you can help someone heal, digging deep within yourself, grabbing hold of your spirit, your life-force, and giving it up, pushing it into them. The same way. You give the ghouls all the goodness, all the life you have inside of you. For some reason that hurts them, burns them. They don't like it. It is one thing that will make them go away, that's for sure." Kerlith explained.

"I see. Anything else?"

"Nothing so far. Nothing else we have tried works. In fact most things we tried somehow bounced back at us. Poison, for example. If you try to well up poison into them, it will only make you sick. But you already know that."

Bel rubbed his temple. "My head is still ringing."

Muolithnon stirred so Kerlith leapt from his chair and went to his side. "I'm here, master."

"Is it still night?" the mage asked groggily.

Kerlith looked out the window and replied. "It's morning, but it grows darker. The eternal night spreads its fingers here now."

"Aye. We must return. See if you can find the horses while I ready myself. Take your stone and be watchful. The ghouls shouldn't return during the day but just the same, don't venture too deep into the forest."

Kerlith retrieved his stone from the table, placed it around his neck and exited the room.

Bel shakily stood, walked across the room and placed himself in front of Nes'egrinon. "Master, I'm truly sorry. Please accept my apology."

"Fifth Year, don't apologize. It makes you look weak and wormy. Maybe like you are, but just the same, don't do it around me. It gives me nausea just thinking about it."

"Yes, master."

"I'm going to tell you two things here. First, I am a mage—"

Bel interrupted him, "I know that. You are one of the great—"

The old man sliced his words in the air with a glare. "I don't care what you think you *know* and who told you what. *I'm* talking here and I'm telling you that I am a mage. Now, along with that comes a certain expectation. People in this uneducated world expect me to know everything about everything. A frog farts in the woods and people around here expect me to know why. But guess what? I don't know why. Maybe the little frog had gas. I don't know. It could have been for any number of reasons. Frogs fart. Get it?"

"Yes, master."

"Don't give me that 'yes, master' line. I'm talking here. What it comes down to is I don't know everything and don't think that you ever will either. Now I was getting to a point but I lost it somewhere. Oh, yeah. Learn this. There is sometimes much more power in inaction than in action."

"I don't understand."

"Of course you don't. We saw that last night. Tell me, what did I do last night to scare them off?"

"You held your staff high and filled it with light. You showed them that you could have destroyed them."

"Did I? Could I have destroyed them?"

"Of course. You are one the greatest mages yet living. They told us at Lasaat—"

"Stop right there because I am starting to think that you really are an idiot. They told you at Lasaat, did they? So that's the garbage Rylith is spreading now. You need to flush all that stuff out of your brain right now."

Bel did not know how to respond so he stood in silence. Rylith, the headmaster at Lasaat—no one there would dare address Rylithnon so, leaving off the last syllable of honor.

The old mage continued, "Listen to me and learn. What I did was a parlor trick. Understand? Psychology. I tricked them. A bright light can no more hurt them than you or I. My bellowing made them think I could so they left. Thank El, they left."

"But..."

"But what?"

"But in the story—it's coming back to me now—in the story of Odysseus, the dead charged at him and his men. The ghouls were desperate for blood but he held them off with his sword."

Muolithnon stumbled from the bed and into the

conversation. "Aye. He did. That sounds about right. A sword of power. A sword full of magic. But it is as your master has said. He speaks truth and you should heed his words. Odysseus could no more hurt the dead with a sword than any of us could last night with mage-light or mage-fire or mage-rain. He tricked them into thinking he could though. Tricking people into thinking that we have more power than we do is one of our best tools. This is why we must not tell anyone how our magic works or what we have the ability to do. They must always think that we have more than we do, that we are merely holding back. There is much power in secrets, young Bel. To destroy the dead? It is not possible. They are dead already."

"Then we are undone," Bel said in defeat.

Nes'egrinon looked at Bel then at Muolithnon and whispered, "No, not yet. There is yet still a way."

Kerlith entered. "Master, I called to your horse using my stone and he came. He looks a little ragged. I think he may have been running to and fro most of the night. If we are to leave today, I don't think we can ride him."

"And your pony?"

Bel interrupted, "He is gone."

"Where?" asked Kerlith.

"The ghoul-kind. Last night. They tore his flesh. I saw it. I don't think he survived."

Kerlith shook then quickly turned his back to them. Muolithnon said, "So the young pony joins the world of the dead. Do not be upset, Kerlith. Perhaps you will see him sooner than you think. But for now we walk. Nes'egrinon, thank you for your hospitality. If the ghouls followed us then I am sorry that I have brought that problem to you. My apprentice and I will go to see what we find. We will send you word, to you and the others, when we find the source of this abomination."

The gray bearded mage looked down at his aged feet, his old hands showing brown spots and his dirty cloak that had already seen too many battles. He peered over at Bel's soft face and frowned. Nes'egrinon looked around his home at his meager possessions and stood slowly. His bones cracked. He turned his head and gazed at Kerlith, standing away from them, still shuddering at the thought of what the ghouls had done to his pony. The old mage stretched out slowly, grabbed his hat from the table, knocked the dust off of it and said with a cracking voice, "Fifth Year, ready yourself. We are walking to the Hinterlands."

Chapter Four

The Hinterlands

Bel wished someone would say something to break the tension but no one spoke and the silence was unnerving. Of course, he couldn't speak first. Not yet. He needed someone to start talking so he could ask a question. He assumed that when he arrived his new master would have spent some time alone with him so that they could talk and the old wizard could explain to him how his training was going to go. But as yet he had no clue as to what his expectations were or even if he could speak openly. At Lasaat, students weren't allowed to speak to masters unless they were in a classroom environment.

It had been dark ever since he got here too and that

was one thing that Bel couldn't quite understand. Bel knew it should be daytime by now. There should be a light-blue sky overhead but all he could see was dark twilight. Sitting on the far horizon behind them streaming fingers of light poked into the darkness, fighting a war for the sky. Bel turned his head back and marveled at it as the group pushed through branches of the overgrown path. Apparently not many people came this way into the wooded Greenlands and Bel could see why. There was nothing here but dark, dense forest; trees, trees, more and more trees, thin but tall, a slender variety of fir, stretching their arms high into the sky.

The silence of the forest was equally disturbing. Much quieter than a peaceful stillness; this was the quiet of death and darkness and eyes watching and patiently waiting. Like a cat crouching in the tall grass waiting for an unknowing sparrow to land just in front of it, Bel felt like a predator's eyes were on him.

Here no bird sang; in this wood, no animal crept. There was only silence and shadows. Bel found himself constantly looking around and over his shoulder at tiny flickers of motion in his periphery, hoping to find insects or snakes or anything really but he could find no motion in the places that he chose to direct his stare.

As Bel and Kerlith walked a few paces behind their teachers, Bel decided to strike up a conversation with his old classmate if for no other reason but to hear his own voice. "So, how's your training going? Been a year already. I see from last night you are already doing some things."

"I've been doing all kinds of stuff. Way better than school. Back there all they let us do was the stupid common stuff. Now I am learning real stone magic under someone who wants to teach me everything."

"Sounds good."

"I have to do some menial stuff too. Take care of my master: food, water, washing, that stuff. But I don't mind because I get to use my stone for all kinds of stuff. It's nothing like school."

"I can't wait." Bel tried to ignore the creeping feeling that something in the woods was watching them, following them and listening to every word they spoke.

"Oh, I got a new stone the other day." Kerlith pulled out the stone hanging from a string around his neck. "Much stronger than the one I had at school. It's onyx but has amethyst surrounding the lower edge. Wicked, right? Here, touch it."

He stared at Bel as they walked, then down at the stone then back at the thin boy. Suddenly Bel realized that the way he said it wasn't so much of an offer as a command. *Touch my stone, now.* "Err, I don't want to touch your stone. It looks good though, I guess. Rocks never interested me much."

Kerlith tucked it back behind his shirt and said, "It's powerful. I can feel it. You have to get yourself some kind of fancy stick, I guess. Get rid of that schoolboy practice staff you're lugging around."

"Sure. Soon as I get a chance. None of this is going how I expected."

"I know. Right. First day in and you're already on an adventure. Well, could be worse. You could be sitting back at his shack cooking dinner every day and learning nothing." Kerlith whispered, "You never can tell with these masters."

Muolithnon began telling a story as they walked, out loud, to no one in particular. "This reminds me of the time that the North King attacked the Hinterlands. We went out on a path such as this one to meet them and let them know that a great mage protected the Land of the stonecutters. After I explained to them who I was and what I was capable of, they went scurrying back to their forest. Such is the power—"

"Wait!" Nes'egrinon held his fist high and turned his head to the side. The party stopped. In the distance they heard hoofs. People were coming on horseback.

A good sign. Ghouls probably do not ride horses, Bel thought.

A group of people came above the ridge, some walking, others on horses and a few draft horses pulling a wagon. They looked ragged and worn. When they arrived, Nes'egrinon said, "Ho! How goes it?"

A man walking said, "Not well. You are the wizard of

the forest, are you not?"

"I am. What can you tell me of what lies ahead? Are there ghoul-kind about?"

"Yes, we are fleeing west. The ghouls have overrun Sha'ul. We waited them out until they broke in and we used torches to burn them but they kept coming. We are the few that are left. The ghouls mostly rest during the day so we were able to steal away."

Kerlith mumbled, "It's dark all the time. I don't see any daylight."

The man looked at Nes'egrinon then at Muolithnon and said bashfully, "If only we had a wizard to protect us."

Nes'egrinon glanced at Muolithnon, then replied, "A few days journey and you should reach the light. You are not far now. Tell me this, what of your dead?"

A young man seated on a horse answered, "We lost so many. It is hard to speak of it. No one is untouched by this sadness. Our dead? Our wives and mothers and fathers and brothers? There is no need to bury them. They usually rise up within hours of dying. Sometimes within minutes. It is painful to speak of it."

"Aye," Muolithnon moaned.

Nes'egrinon's face grew somber as if he was thinking of another time. "I am sorry for you and your people. I will not hold you longer, only answer me one last thing. Tell me, does it take only one bite?"

The man swept the dirt with his foot and said, "My

wife, she tried to help. I told her to stay inside. Only one bite took her. The poison crept into her and she died. The children too. Others tried to fight it. The stronger ones. They went into a fever that lasted days in some but none have survived it. None I've seen."

"I am sorry to hear this."

The young man on the horse added, "One odd thing though, the children did not rise. They died and when they didn't rise for some time, we buried them."

Nes'egrinon's brow furrowed. "Oh, is that so?"

The man said, "Yes, that is something that we have yet to explain. I suppose there are many things we cannot explain. Not everyone rises. Some just die and are gone. Especially the children. I would like to think they go somewhere else but then why did my wife rise? I do not like to think about it. I just want to flee this darkness and forget, if I can, all that I have seen."

"Thank you and Godspeed."

The group departed and Kerlith lit his stone with mage-light. Later the others did also, Muolithnon his mage-stone and Nes'egrinon and Bel their staffs of mage-wood. It was getting darker the deeper they traveled and the closer they came to the Hinterlands. They all seemed to unconsciously quicken their steps as the dark and the dread surrounded them.

Muolithnon began telling another one of his tales. "This reminds me of the time I battled a swamp creature.

It was wooded like this and dark but after I lit my stone full of power he could do nothing but run as fast as he could. He was never seen again."

The forest was silent except for an occasional distant rustling and the four were on edge. Bel pushed hard from within himself and lit his staff brighter. It made him feel safer to be able to see deep into the forest although he knew that that was a lie. He wasn't safe at all.

"Fifth Year. Stop burning your energy like a fool. If a battle comes you will need it. Shine your light as dim as possible. We don't want to attract any unwanted attention anyway."

There was a swish and a thump as an arrow struck the ground just in front of them. A group of men on horseback sat at the top of the path staring them down. They were shadowed in darkness.

"What?" Muolithnon squeaked then he motioned for them to quickly leave the path. They all dashed to the safety of the forest but they could not go in too deep as the wood, full of slender and tightly knit trees, became thick and brushy. Shouting was behind them. More arrows rained in. Kerlith and Bel crouched low and they all extinguished their mage-lights. An arrow twanged into the brush next to them.

Nes'egrinon spit out, "Bandits!" then placed his hands upon two adjacent trees, an oak and an elm, and mumbled words that Bel could not make out. The forest became darker and twisted as if they were somehow moving.

The old mage released his hands and breathed hard, staring at the ground, exhausted. Bel listened to the old man gasp and felt sorry for him for he seemed to tire so quickly. He was said to once be one of the greatest wizards in all of the known lands. They told us at Lasaat, anyway. Bel remembered the tales. He was the man who rescued the rightful king of Argus from exile and built the outer ring of defense that surrounded Lasaat; the only person who knew the length and breadth of the Black Forest from the glacier edge to the far river; the only one who had spoken with a dragon and lived. It was even rumored that he knew Achilles and fought against the Akkadians. But now? He is tired, old and—how does the saying go?—one foot in the grave and the other on a banana peel? No, he is not long for this world and what is to become of me when he dies?

The group emerged from the wood but the path looked different. "Where are we?" Bel asked without thinking but then wished he had kept quiet. He still did not know if it was his place to speak openly yet.

Muolithnon twisted his back and shakily said, "Kerlith?"

Kerlith turned to see an arrow trembling in his master's shoulder. He reached up and snapped off the feathered end of the shaft as the mage gasped then winced and said, "Push it through."

The arrowhead emerged bloody with chunks of flesh. Kerlith instinctively held his hand over the wound and pushed in healing.

Muolithnon rose to his feet and announced, "That will do for now. We must keep moving. There is no time for bandages. If Sha'ul is overrun as they say, then there will be no safety there. We must reach Sha'la or one of the other villages before nightfall. We must get inside the walls."

Kerlith said, "Lawlessness has fallen upon the land. It is as foretold."

His master replied, "Aye." He looked about in both directions on the pathway then asked, "Master Archmage, you have transported us. Which way now?"

Nes'egrinon looked in front of them for a while then turned around and looked back. He turned around and looked in front again and scratched his head. He turned around once more then said, "Err... this way. Yes. This way then."

Bel looked at Kerlith who looked back and shrugged. They walked on the darkening path for what seemed like a half-day's journey without the least change of scenery. Then the lane became narrower as the elm and pine and fir thickened; branches swatted them as they forced their way through. The roadway had clearly ended but they each knew the truth that no one wanted to say; there was no turning back now. After they pushed through a large crop of trees they came to a small cliff edge with a river below.

"Now what?" Muolithnon exclaimed somewhat desperately as it was getting darker; the dim twilight was fading to black.

The elder mage pulled down his gray hood, revealing his scarred face. His eyes were dark and impartial. They did not pierce or accuse but there was some hidden fire deep within them as if he had seen and known things that no other man could know. He said plainly, "You can jump if you like," and stepped backwards off the cliff falling into the rapidly flowing current below.

Bel looked then quickly leapt after him, eager to prove himself. Kerlith grabbed his master's arm and looked at his face to see if he might need help. The mage nodded to his apprentice and they stepped off together.

The freezing stream carried them a short distance as they swam to the far side then exited on to a grassy bank at the valley of sparsely covered hills. Several stamped-in trails led up and away and Nes'egrinon looked at each one in turn, rubbing his chin with a perplexed look on his face. A path through high grass, another through low, a trail between thickets and a twisting row down and up ravines and stony hills; paths, paths, paths everywhere and not a sign of civilization or a recent footprint; nobody, nobody, not even the smallest twig broken to indicate anyone had been through here in a long, long time. He said, "This one," pointing, seemingly at random, at the steepest then immediately began walking up it, using the small bushes as handholds, dragging himself uphill. Bel stepped behind him. Muolithnon and Kerlith both wrung out their outer coverings then followed.

A long time passed where all they did was climb up and down hills and each time they scaled one more ominous than the last, Nes'egrinon said, "It should be just over this next ridge."

Bel shivered and his hands were torn from clawing up the hills. It was perpetually dark now and there was no way to know exactly what time it was but it was getting cold. It must be near to midnight if it was not already. Ghouls would come if they stayed in one place too long; they had to keep moving.

After a time of climbing and descending Bel smelled something different and he furrowed his brow. A soft, curious scent danced on Bel's nose. Kerlith noticed it also. When Nes'egrinon saw the puzzled looks on their faces, he said, "Spicewood. We are almost there. Should be just over this next ridge."

The pathway grew wider, wide enough for four men to walk abreast and they entered a dark tunnel of Spicewood branches holding hands above them. The trail curved in a meandering way, through the trees, through the silent forest without the sound of birds or rabbits or other small animals. Lost were the sounds, the rustling, the chirping and singing, the indications that they were walking through a living, breathing forest. All that surrounded them was the silence of death. As the thoroughfare peeked over the ridge it opened into a clearing and rough stone steps that led to a small shelter of dark, moss-covered bark, not much smaller than Nes'egrinon's own home.

The old man said, "Ahh. Here we are. See? A shelter. We will stay here tonight."

Muolithnon looked at him questioningly but said nothing and entered the shack whose door hung open.

A few moments later he stepped back out and said, "It will have to do. I'll cast an enchantment."

The old mage said, "No, I'll do it. Go in and rest. Kerlith, start a fire. Fifth Year, can you help him? We're still in the forest. This is my charge. I'll take care of our protection spell." After the events of the day, no one could protest. They were all exhausted.

It was a strange structure and it struck Bel as odd that such large logs were used to form its walls. But it would keep them safe from ghouls. There was a pile of wood ready near the hearth so they could warm up and dry off too. And maybe they would sleep. Maybe. The building was constructed of large round logs standing on end and supporting a roof of slats. The cracks between them were stuffed with twigs and a mud-like mixture. Inside sat a table and two chairs and not much else, but the dirt floor in front of the fire looked very comfortable right now.

As they prepared the fire, Kerlith baited, "Something's wrong with you."

"Why?"

"Your master doesn't say much to you. I'm guessing the old wizard can detect your incompetence?"

Bel did not return his gaze. "Shut up, fool. He will when he gets the chance."

"I'm just saying what I'm seeing."

"Listen Kerlith, we started this trip nice and all and I haven't brought up our history back at the University so I was just going to let that go. But if you start acting ignorant with your stupid comments like you did back when we were kids then we are going to have a problem."

Kerlith chuckled and didn't respond.

Muolithnon slumped down next to Kerlith and Bel, leaning his back against the single center post, and crowed, "Now this reminds me of the time that South Be'ershore was overrun with marauders. When I showed up to save them they were all huddled in a shack much like this one. Of course I had to save them, the poor pathetic lot. I always take care of the little people."

Bel, wanting no more of Muolithnon's stories, went outside, stood on the front steps and looked up at the sky. It spooked him for a moment when he didn't see any stars in the blackness but he quickly realized that the eternal night, whatever it was, would eat all forms of light, not just daylight. The sky was pitch black. There was not a star in the sky.

Nes'egrinon completed his enchantment and climbed the stairs to stand next to Bel and look out into the woods. "Do you hear that?" the old mage asked creakily.

Bel focused his hearing. He heard nothing initially then noticed a sound in the distance. It sounded like the ocean. Bel recalled his childhood in Lavaala; he could always hear the crashing waves of the ocean from his home and it reminded him that his father was out there somewhere. The noise was kind of like that, but somehow different; it was a kind of soft roaring, like ocean but also somehow like wind. It was the kind of noise that was subtle enough to fall into the background din. "Is that... the ocean? Are we close to the ocean?"

"It is not the ocean. The ocean is far away. Guess again." The old man said.

Bel tried to not think about it and it quickly disappeared, as if it was hiding. Bel focused again, trying to detect what could possibly be causing the sound and it became louder as he listened attentively. The young apprentice looked at the leaves on the trees and saw that they did not stir. "I don't know. It sounds like wind but the leaves do not stir."

"Wind? Indeed. It is wind. But not the kind you think of. The air is still." Nes'egrinon looked over at Bel and answered the question that he did not ask. "Reach out. Touch. Reach out with your mind, your spirit; touch that which is still living. Tell me what you find."

Bel calmed his spirit and closed his eyes. He sent out his spirit, calling, calling to all that was living, looking for an answer to a question that he could not ask. He had done this before, many times in fact, looking for life, calling for the light to come to him, other times looking for information. He used it often during the old apprentice game of hide and seek. They would all hide then ask the animals where the others were. Sometimes they would let them look through their eyes. But this was entirely different. There were no questions to ask, just a feeling.

He sent out his mind and the roaring grew louder and louder and became a sort of howling. There were sounds in the forest, moving sounds, rustling sounds; Bel could feel them now, but this was none of those; the howl was inside his own head. It was the kind of sound that could drive a man insane if he listened to it long enough.

"Madness," Bel coughed involuntarily.

"Yes!" the mage said excitedly. "Yes, it is the sound of madness. It is here, in the dark, waiting for us. Be mindful of it." Without another word he went inside leaving Bel alone with his thoughts.

Bel listened, trying to understand the noise, trying to understand how the sound could be in his head. The wail grew fiercer the longer he listened to it. He remembered a storm, full of wind and salt and gale, smashing against the side of the house as if it would throw it to the ground like so many sticks, long before he left Lavaala. He was young, just a boy at his mother's knees. She cried for the storm and his older brother told her everything would be all right and Bel did not understand until later. His father was out on the water.

The roaring grew stronger, ecstatic, excited, as if a hunting dog found his scent and was calling out to the others, "Come! I have found them! Here! Here! Here! They are here! Follow me! I have their scent! Let's get them! Attack!"

Bel stared straight ahead, into the black, suddenly trying to squeeze the clamoring, shrieking sound out of his mind, trying to beat it back. Get out! Get out! Get out of my mind! He stared into the darkness of the forest, shaking, and he could see nothing, but in his periphery he caught glimpses of motion, something in the shadows, and he knew it was something more than ghouls. It was like when he was on the path but now he refused to chase his eyes around after them. He was terrified. He knew they could not reach him—there was an enchantment—but they were somehow in his mind. He couldn't stop shaking. He knew they would not be there when he looked. He knew where they really were and it was all he could do to keep himself from going insane.

Chapter Five

Ghoul Speak

The four slept on the dirt floor huddled near the fire. Bel slept fitfully and awoke restless. There was nothing to eat in the abandoned home so Muolithnon took the situation into his own hands. "Kerlith, we are hungry. See if you can call a few pigeons. Or rabbits. Mmmmm, that would be good for a stew."

Kerlith bounced up and headed out the door. Bel looked at Nes'egrinon and the old wizard only said, "Fifth Year, ready the pot. Find some water so we can boil whatever the apprentice brings back."

Bel went outside and looked around. There was a woodpile behind the structure and most of it was still usable. The house couldn't have been abandoned for too long. Next to the woodpile was a small three-walled shed with some crude tools and next to that was a hand-pump well. Bel retrieved a pail from the shed and began pumping but nothing came out but dust. Bel retrieved his staff, waved it above the pump and called to the water until it came.

Hunger didn't bother Bel. He was quite used to it, being a fisherman's son on the western coast. Becoming a wizard was never about becoming rich or having a full belly. He wanted to help people. People like the fishermen in his village, people who no one ever seemed to want to help. Their home was shored up enough to keep out the storms, barely, and they had more than many, a small boat, a couple of nets and a gaff. Bel had his own knife that he used to cut crustaceans off the rocks for soup when his father was gone for days. They had much and much to be thankful for. He wondered how his family fared without him.

By the time Bel had the pot full of water coming to a boil, Kerlith returned with four fine-looking rabbits and two pigeons. It would be a feast. As they ate, Nes'egrinon said, "Now that's the best rabbit I've had in ages. We will stay here until Muolithnon has regained his strength. Maybe a few days. You can get us more rabbits, right?"

Night came slowly and even though the day was as dark as night, something changed in the air, and all of them felt it change, when it would be too dangerous to venture away from the safety of the home. Bel sat out on the front steps with Kerlith, both staring into the forest, Bel trying to understand what happened the previous evening, Kerlith's mind pondering their future journey. Kerlith shivered as the night air grew colder. Then the howling came.

Bel asked, "Do you hear that?"

Kerlith blinked hard then said, "I don't hear anything. What? You going crazy? Hearing things? It's getting cold out here. I'm going inside."

The roaring grew louder even though Bel wasn't listening for it, wasn't seeking it. In fact he was trying to block it out. Bel stood and involuntarily stepped backwards until his back was against the wall and fought the shriek with all his might. Then the ghouls came.

They stepped out of the forest and walked calmly towards him, a young man and two women. They were dressed like forest people except they were all gray: their skin, their clothing, everything about them was a dull, dusty gray. They walked up to the edge of the steps, just to the border of the enchantment. Bel knew they couldn't see past it but somehow they knew he was there.

"Hello? Hello in there?" the dead man croaked as if his throat was full of dust.

Bel did not respond.

Groggily, the dead man said, "Please. We mean you no harm. This is my family. This was our home. Please, we just want to talk."

Bel walked to the edge of the enchantment. The male ghoul's face was inches from his.

"Please, we mean you no harm. Look at us. See? See? Look at these women. I know you are in there. Please." He strained to get the words out.

Bel knew the enchantment would hold them back. They were dead; they could not reach him. If they were living, breathing human beings, they could walk right up the stairs and step into the house. But the dead could not. Bel knew he could turn around and walk away. He could go inside. But something was pulling on him, something was still raging in his mind.

The ghoul-kind turned despondently and began to walk away when Bel said, "Wait!"

The group stopped and turned around.

Bel said nervously, "Step back. Step back a few feet."

The dead man motioned to the others then Bel stepped outside of the enchantment and stood on the final step of the house. He dared not venture further.

The gray-skinned man strained. "Please. A few drops of blood. Please, just a few drops."

"You will answer my questions? Then, when I say, you will leave?"

"Yes."

Bel took out his knife and cut the tip of his finger and squeezed a few drops of blood onto the dirt.

"More. More, please," One of the women groaned.

"Come forward one at a time," Bel said holding out his knife in front of him.

The woman who spoke stepped forward slowly and stood in front of Bel. He cut his finger a little more, let the blood cover the knife and held it out toward the dead woman. She licked the knife eagerly. As she licked it color ran into her cheeks, then her face, then her clothing. A calm swept over her and the darkness left her eyes. She seemed almost... normal, almost human.

"Ask. Ask what you will. I will answer what I know."

"Tell me who you are. What happened to you? How did you become like this?"

"My husband is there. The other woman is my sister. My children... we have not found them yet. Last winter we aided a traveler. He was sick. When my sister also became sick my husband sent him away. He didn't want the sickness to spread to the children but it was too late. We lost my dear Kith, Tor and Bel a few weeks later. Then my sister died too."

"I share your child's name. My name is Bel also. I'm sorry for you."

The woman smiled softly then continued, "There was no healer in these lands and with the weather the way it was, we could not travel. We buried the children and my sister behind the woodshed." She looked back at her briefly.

"And you two?"

"My husband and I were a mere shadow of our former selves after the children died. We wanted to leave, to forget this place, but where would we go? When the ghoul-kind came, they promised that we would see the children if we joined them, if we gave them our blood. How could we refuse?"

The gray began to spread into the woman as she sadly turned and walked back to the others. The other woman took her place.

Bel cut himself again and held out his knife. The woman quickly consumed the blood and gasped as color poured into her frame. She smiled widely.

"Hello Bel. My name is Shii. What would you know of me?"

"What do you know of this?" Bel waved his hands at them as he asked it. "What do you know of the ghouls? Why do they wander openly? How did this come to be?"

Shii looked perplexed. "This I do not know exactly. I died from the wasting disease, as my sister said, and when I died I found myself in the underworld, the land of the dead. I do not know if you know this but the dead don't talk to each other too much. One day—oh, old habits die hard, I suppose—one day? Hahaha. In the land of the dead there is no day. No night. No time really. It is all just one continuous moment. It is eternity. Yes, eternity because there is no such thing as time there. It is hard to think of, no? How can you, who has never been there, understand such a concept?"

"You're right. I don't understand."

"No matter. What I mean to say is that suddenly there was time! Suddenly something happened. I don't know what it was or why. All I can say is that I was drawn to it, inexplicably. It was time. Somehow, someway, time had invaded the world of the dead. I walked towards it. We all did. Well, most of us anyway; some feared it and stayed back. But we were all drawn to it. I walked out into it and through it and came here. I came back to my home."

"What was it? What was drawing you?"

"I don't know. But when we got there, to the breach —I don't know what it was but that is what we called it— when we got to the breach, I stepped through and eventually I made my way here."

"So not everyone came through? Why did they fear? What scared them?"

"Everyone? No. Not hardly. Do you know how many dead there are? In all of time? Think about it. That was a silly question." The color in the woman's face began to drain before she could finish and her smile left. She glanced down at the knife and the blood on it. Bel could see the desire in her face but she still turned and joined the others.

Finally the man stepped forward and licked the blood from Bel's knife. Brightness entered his cheeks.

Bel asked, "Where are the ghouls now? What is their

plan? Does anyone rule them? Is there a leader?"

The man frowned. "A leader? Not that I have seen. The dead are people, just like you, only dead. We were once living and we know what it means to be alive. Perhaps you can feel it now. You are a wizard in training are you not? I can tell; I met one once before. Perhaps you can feel it? The desire? The desire for life? It is in all living things. All living things love life. All that are sane anyway. And this exists with the dead also, only it is amplified. We love life more than you can know. One day you will understand."

The man paused as the color in his cheeks faded to gray, wanting more blood, wanting more life, but knowing there was no more to be had here he turned around and joined the two women. Bel stepped back behind the shelter of the enchantment and watched them wander back into the wood slowly.

Bel contemplated all that he heard. He felt that they did not answer his questions but he knew much more and he thought it was worth the risk. Bel went behind the enchantment and pulled the door open to the home. Nes'egrinon was walking across the room just a few steps away. Bel thought that he might have been standing at the door just now. Maybe listening. But he couldn't be sure. The other two were already asleep in front of the fire.

Bel slept quickly and dreamed vividly of a boy with one arm, standing on the edge of darkness, surrounded by ghoul-kind, him calling out to him. The boy spoke, "Don't trust him. He is a liar. He is lying to you. Watch him closely and do not trust him." Bel shook the image of the boy from his mind when he woke but it troubled him.

The next day was slow and long but Muolithnon seemed a bit better. That night the roaring came again, calling Bel out, trying to drive him insane but it had less power over him than the previous two nights. He didn't know if he was becoming accustomed to it or perhaps it was not so close tonight or maybe it had given up on him. Or maybe it was working, maybe he was going insane. Do the insane know when they are insane? Do they know when it happens, when is the exact moment that they lose their minds? After he fought with the howl in his mind he stumbled indoors to try to sleep. Nes'egrinon looked at him curiously but said nothing. Bel almost wondered whether his master was really waiting on Muolithnon's healing or on something entirely different. They had plenty of time to talk in these last few days but his master said nothing to him. Was he watching me? Testing me? Maybe if I make some terrible mistake he will reject me?

Although they hadn't really done anything in this shelter, Bel felt tired. He placed himself next to Kerlith and Muolithnon, trying to lie close enough to share their body warmth. The dream came quickly.

His silhouette stood out from the black. Bel walked towards him to get a better look but somehow he already knew whom he was, the one-armed boy. Bel stopped a few feet away and waited for him to look up. Odd how I can see him at all in the darkness, Bel thought.

The one-armed boy looked up and said, "You didn't listen. I told you. Why don't you listen?"

"What? I don't understand."

"He's lying to you."

"Who?"

The one-armed boy was about Bel's age, about his size and weight too. They even looked a bit alike. They could be brothers.

"You're not too bright are you?" The one-armed boy turned slowly and Bel couldn't keep his eyes from staring at the empty socket where there should have been an arm much like his own. It was a burnt hole. The boy stepped slowly in front of him and extended his arm at Bel and suddenly a glowing staff appeared in his hand.

Bel awoke with a start, sweating, and huffed, "He was an apprentice!"

Chapter Six

Sha'ane Village

"Aye, I feel strong," Muolithnon said.

Nes'egrinon stood creakily and said with disappointment in his voice, "No more rabbit then. I guess we have to walk."

Kerlith hopped up and grabbed his few belongings.

The image of the one-armed boy still burned in Bel's mind as he gathered up his cloak and his short staff and headed out the door. The group stepped out from behind the spell of protection and Bel felt the eyes of the forest on him. He spied three sets of red glowing dots just at the edge of the tree line and he knew who they were, the dead from the other night, waiting, still looking for their lost children, their lost, dead children. For some reason Bel thought that they would never find them.

Kerlith lit his stone and took lead. As they left the small clearing Nes'egrinon waived his staff and the spell of protection dissipated behind them. They walked.

The path looped round in meandering directions, always turning around obstacles, huge boulders or trees, natural outcropping of poisonous vegetation or areas that probably were populated with predators. The roadway looked used anyway. That's good, Bel thought. We're closer to some civilization. Although people are what attracts the ghoul-kind too. The blood of people anyway. There will be more ghouls here.

As they walked in the dark, Bel quizzed, probing his new master's temperament, "Master? Might I ask a question?"

He did not look back. "You just did."

Bel paused, wondering if he should just go ahead and blurt it out. "Master? The trees. Their leaves. I saw them in the twilight the other day. They are the color of blood."

"Yes, they are."

"Why, Master? Does the darkness kill the trees too?" Bel had never seen any other than green leaves.

By the dim light of his mage-stone, Kerlith looked back at Bel as if he was wondering the same thing.

Nes'egrinon spoke. "Where there is no life, there is no light. You know this, don't you?"

"Every First Year knows this."

"There is a big difference between being told to

memorize something and knowing it. I did not ask you if you had heard the phrase before but if you *knew* it."

Bel didn't know what to say.

Nes'egrinon continued, "More on that later. For now, let's assume you can't pick out a monkey from a line up with a table and a banana. Okay?"

"Err… okay."

"So this is pretty elementary metaphysics. Where there is no life there is no light. Yes? Right? All things have life and light in them. All things that are living. And all things must be constantly fed light, for creatures that are living consume life in order to survive. Do you understand?"

"Yes, Master. But the trees—"

"Stop the jaw-jawing. Listen and learn. That's the problem with you kids today. Always wanting to talk. Just listen. You have life in you. All of us do. And what you have learned from that school… What have they taught you of this? They have taught you to use the light around you, yes?"

"Yes Master, but—"

"But now there is no life around you. Only death. Only darkness. Only emptiness. So where will your light come from?"

"From… inside?" Bel offered.

"Right. Be wary. Be careful. Do not give too much of your light lest you extinguish your own life."

Bel waited for a while and said, "Master, then the trees. They are dying, and this is why their leaves bleed?"

"They are not being fed life. What else could they do? The leaves are red. Soon they will turn brown. Then hard. Then crumple and fall away." The mage's voice cracked as he said it. He loved the forest.

An old man, a young man and two youths trudged through the forest in the dark, only able to see a short distance in front of them by a dimming mage-light cast from a single stone. They footslogged along surrounded by only the sounds of their breathing. Bel tried to look down but could not see his hands, or his chest, or any part of him. He felt like a floating spirit, moved along by the force of breeze, cast to and fro like a jellyfish in the ocean near his childhood home of Lavaala. He could not see or sense the ground in front of him but only placed his feet forward, step by step, in blind faith that there actually existed an earth to walk upon.

As they continued on, Muolithnon said "Do you hear that?" and they all stopped.

Nes'egrinon pushed to the front and said, "We are close to a village. Sounds like it is just past that ridge."

They walked slowly over the ridge and looking down the path saw a clearing and just beyond it, a small village lit by torches.

"No," Muolithnon exhaled. "It doesn't have any walls. There is no rest here."

Nes'egrinon squinted at the younger mage in the dim light and continued walking. There was a group of people in the clearing with hand torches and they were surrounding what looked to be two ghouls. The four stepped into the clearing, just at the edge of the group with torches and the old mage motioned for them to wait. The pathway was downtrodden and beaten. The smell of wet mud and rank, wet grass pervaded their nostrils.

"Wait! Please! You don't understand!" cried one being surrounded by the townsfolk with torches. He was not a ghoul, Bel realized.

"Wait? For what?" Cried out a brawny man. "So you can let *them* in?" The man pointed his torch hard at the second person in the circle. A woman.

"Just let her go! Let her go back into the forest," said another man with a torch.

"Aye," said the large man. "And send him with her."

Nes'egrinon stepped out of the darkness. "Hello, friends. We are weary travelers. Might we find shelter here?"

The men with torches turned toward him and the large man swung his torch closer. "What manner of men are you coming out of this forest? Ghoul-kind?"

The old mage replied, "We are men, like other men. Just men."

"Aye," Muolithnon added. "We have come through the forest and the darkness. We seek only shelter for a short time and we will be on our way. We have coin to pay."

"Who has need of coin when the likes of these be about." The large man spat at the woman in the circle.

Kerlith followed the two mages closely. Bel felt like they were walking into a powder keg and wondered if they might be safer in the forest.

"What are their crimes, if I might ask?" Muolithnon asked.

A younger man spoke quickly, before the large one could start, "The woman, she committed no crime. She is dead. One of the ghoul-kind who now walks these parts. The man, he is her husband. He's been feeding her his blood. Keeping her in his room, in the inn—"

The large man interrupted, "Right under our noses!" He swung the torch near the man and dead woman. "Can you believe it? He's been keeping this dead woman in his room and feeding her his blood! Then, every night, all her friends come a calling, looking for more to feed on and him the whole time pretending that she isn't in his room calling out to them."

"No!" the man cried out, shaking. "She's my wife! She wouldn't do that! Those others that came, they're not like her. They're... animals." The man began to cry.

Muolithnon mumbled to Nes'egrinon, "Odd one we've stepped into, huh?"

The old mage stepped forward and said, "Good

people. My name is Nes'egrinon."

Several of the torchbearers stepped back quickly.

Nes'egrinon continued, "Perhaps you have heard of me."

One muttered, "The wizard of the forest."

"Good mage, if only you had been here some days ago, before this started. We have lost so many," another man added.

Another said, "Welcome, good mage, to Sha'ane."

Nes'egrinon looked at the village with a sudden sadness, "Sha'ane? Yes, it is. I have been here before. It has been a long, long time. I had forgotten."

One said, "Yes, yes. My great grandfather spoke of you fondly and often, especially just before he died. His memory was leaving him and he could only remember the old times, the times so many here would forget, the times of war and starvation. He said you saved us."

"That was a long time ago."

Another said, "Master, what should we do with one such as this?"

The old wizard looked at the two carefully then replied, "First, I would speak to them both."

The circle broke and the men with torches stepped back. The large man did not step back too far though.

"Thank you, good mage. Thank you for saving me." The man bowed deep in front of Nes'egrinon.

"Do not thank me yet. I need information."

"Yes, anything."

"Give your wife some blood. I would speak to her."

The man had many cuts on his hands and his arms. He found a spot which was yet unwounded and cut it shallowly with his knife while the gray ghoul that he called his wife looked on eagerly. She drank deeply and her flesh gained a pinkish hue. She wiped the red from her lips and turned to the archmage. Smiling, she said, "What would you know of me?"

"Tell me of your kind. How do you communicate?"

"We are dead. There is no communication among us. Without blood, we are mostly silent anyway."

"And what of this claim. That you call to them."

Her husband blurted out, "It's not true!"

"Hold." The old wizard showed the man his palm.

The dead woman spoke, "I cannot. There are others though, among the dead, wizards of old, seers, speakers of the future, others with powers, those of whom I know little. Perhaps they can do as you ask."

"And are there any such as these in the forest around us?"

"Yes. I believe so, yes. Some days ago, when I was in the forest, I heard of one who spoke things, things that he could not know for certain. He said that four wizards were coming. And now here you are." The smile left her face as the pinkish tint faded to dull gray. The woman looked longingly at her husband's bandaged arm.

The archmage stepped back to council with Muolithnon, "So, what do you think?"

"It is a tough one, it is. For me, keep the villagers happy. We would like to stay here, would we not?"

"Well said."

To the man Nes'egrinon motioned. "What would you do? Go with your wife, or stay here? You cannot do both."

The man looked lovingly at his dead wife's gray face and choked out, "I have no reason to live without her. I will go to the forest."

Bel's face fell as the two walked out. Kerlith smiled for some reason. The other torchbearers returned to the village. The large man spat then turned away.

Nes'egrinon said, "Come. Let us find our way to an inn."

Chapter Seven

The Mayor Of Sha'ane

Bel's eyes snapped open and for a moment he had to think about exactly where he was. *In the inn. In our room.* He heard screams coming from beyond the door. They sounded distant yet he was sure they were from somewhere in the building. The young man slowly reached back behind him trying to determine if Kerlith was still in the bed. He wasn't. Bel rolled over in the darkness and felt around. The spot Kerlith was in wasn't even warm. He had been gone for some time. Bel sat up and tried to look around but couldn't make out much.

"Phos," Bel softly spoke the language of the ancients,

calling for light to come into the room. He half expected nothing to happen in this land of eternal darkness but some light flickered into the room from under the door. Bel felt badly about calling it, knowing that it's source was probably the life-force of one of the villagers in the inn. He was burning a moment of that person's life only so that he could see in the dark room, taking a tiny portion of life in a place where it so was so precious and rare. The dim light flickered and danced and Bel hurriedly looked around, trying to locate his staff as he did not want to have to call in more light. Neither Nes'egrinon nor Muolithnon were in the room either. Their bed was turned down but empty.

"Robsos," Bel called out to his staff, suddenly worried since he could not immediately locate it. It was not where he left it. The staff bounced from below a small pile of clothing and bounded up into his hand.

Bel stood and let the light enter the tip of his staff. The screams outside of his room grew louder. He walked to the door, opened it and stepped out. Standing on the elevated walkway Bel looked down upon the dining area of the inn. The four of them had eaten there before they retired to their room the night before. Nes'egrinon had seemed pensive but enjoyed the roast duck. Kerlith sat eagerly at his master's side and goaded Muolithnon into telling "just one more story" for the barmaids and locals. Of course his master needed no such motivation to tell another tale of his greatness.

Now there were ghouls attempting to feast upon human flesh and not a wizard to be found anywhere. A ghoul charged the bartender, diving over the bar and tackling him. Another set of ghouls surrounded a woman, the barmaid from last night, she on one side of a table and the two on the other. They were each moving from opposite sides, giving her no way of escape. Another ghoul, a woman, was bent over a table and draining the blood from a small child. She stopped and began crying as her flesh became bright and lively then cried out, "No! The blood lust! I have killed mine own sweet Tor!" She ran, slamming herself into a wall, then out of the room screaming. Tucked into a corner was a man, hiding, riddled with fear. Bel was mesmerized by the scene.

"Blood!" one of the ghoul-kind howled out from just down the aisle from Bel. It startled him. He quickly turned towards the voice and pulled healing into his body. As the ghoul charged towards him, grabbing his shoulders, the two tumbled forward and Bel fell. The ghoul quickly leapt back screaming, "Aaarrgh!" The creature looked down at himself and seeing his gray flesh quickly turn mottled and black, ran down the steps and out the door. The rest of the ghoul-kind looked up at Bel as he stood and addressed them, "Leave now or I'll do the same to you!"

Most of them began to exit. Bel crept down the

staircase and looked at the bloody table and the body of a small child. Sucking sounds came the bar area. Bel quickly drew life-energy into himself and stepped behind the bar to see a ghoul squatted over the fallen bartender.

"Thulo," Bel said, commanding the ghoul to leave.

"Make me," replied the gray fiend without turning around to see whom he was addressing.

The bartender appeared to be dead. Bel reached deep in his belly and pushed hard. He pushed forth life and light and goodness, channeling it into his arm. He stretched forth his hand to the dead man and attempted to place his palm on his forehead. The dead man swung his head around and bit Bel's hand but where his teeth touched Bel's skin, smoke erupted. The gray-skinned man released his bite and slumped back.

"How?" the ghoul exclaimed, rubbing his mouth with his hand.

"Thulo, I said."

The ghoul looked down at his victim and back at Bel with a snarl of disgust then slid himself over the bar and quickly exited the room.

Bel shook the bartender who coughed hard. He was not dead. Yet. The young mage in training helped the man to stand.

"He was my partner," The bartender said. "One of the first to go."

Bel, seeing bite marks on the man's chest, placed his

hand over them and pushed in healing, hoping that it would be enough, hoping that the man would not join the dead in the forest. The man gasped hard as life entered him.

"He hated me. Thought I cheated him out of a sum of money. I didn't. Honestly. I didn't. Even in death, he cannot forgive. But I am innocent."

Bel stood and left the man, walking toward the exit doors and the screams and moans and unknown chaos. Bel adjusted his shirt at the door, grabbed his breath and mumbled, "Okay. Let's do this," and opened the door and stepped out.

Nes'egrinon, Muolithnon and Kerlith were all in the street battling the ghoul-kind. The young man and his master had their hands on their mage-stones, blue and red lights swirling around them. The old wizard simply stood near them calmly. Some villagers were heaving oil from the second floors of their buildings. Others were throwing torches, trying to burn the creatures. Many of the dead, the more aggressive ones, ran from the surrounding forest into the village, attacking as they ran and continuing back into the forest in a loop. It was a constant stream of bestial ghouls whooping, screaming, swinging their arms and weapons, thirsty for blood. Most of the other ghoul-kind held back at the forest edge, watching like spectators, perhaps waiting for the town's defenses to fail, the longing for blood on their faces mixed with a sort of guilty embarrassment at what they knew they were being driven to do. Bel realized that these were the simple townsfolk, recently dead, not wanting to become marauders like the others but yet still driven by the desire for blood, the desire for life. It was something that they could not escape. The others, the ones attacking, were, by their behavior and dress, the town outlaws, drunks and thieves. They howled, leapt, spun and made terrible, angry faces. How good could they expect their behavior to be in death considering how it was during their lifetimes? It is these evil dead that are the problem, Bel thought. If we can be rid of them, the others will not attack.

Bel called life into his staff and was surprised to see wisps of light flickering out of the surrounding villagers chests, some from the second floor balconies, and quickly gathering into the head of his staff. Bel said to himself, "This is real. This is real. This is what I have been training for the last six years. I am about to get into the real action. I am not a Fifth Year anymore. I am an apprentice. I am going to do this." He stepped off the front porch and headed towards the others in the center of the roadway, uncertainty still shaking through his frame.

Nes'egrinon glanced over at Bel. "Fifth Year, quickly. Join us here. We want the ghoul-kind to focus their attacks on us. To keep the villagers out of the line of fire. They will be drawn to our mage-blood."

He skipped over to them and held his staff high. He

was nervous. He was shaking. But he was really excited. He knew the dead would stream toward them. No one knew why but ghoul-kind could smell mage-blood. And for some reason when one of the dead drank the blood of a mage, the effect lasted much, much longer. All the dead would want to drink the blood of the masters and Bel and Kerlith were standing next to these two giant targets.

What to do? What to do? What to do? Bel knew that healing worked. Kerlith had told him as much and now he had seen it with his own eyes and by his own hands. But it was risky because he would have to touch the ghoul and he could only reliably do it to one at a time. Of course there was the trick that his master did, tricking the ghoul-kind into thinking that he could destroy them all with a word. But how long would that last? The villagers seemed to be doing all right with fire though. The ghouls were certainly susceptible to it. As soon as they caught fire they would immediately run back into the forest, screaming their dead heads off. Several trails of fire and burning ghoul entrails could be seen streaming into the forest. It smelled none too nice either.

A handful popped out from behind the edge of a wall and charged them. They were close, too close and running at them in a full gallop. Nes'egrinon slammed his staff into the ground, sending out a tremor, collapsing the group to the ground. Kerlith stumbled then latched onto Bel's shoulder and braced himself, nearly falling down in the quake.

"Come! Let's go!" howled the leader of the small band, pulling the arms of one of the others up and pointing toward the mages but the others retreated.

"Let's see how much longer that works," Muolithnon muttered under his breath.

Just then, a dead man leapt off a roof just over the young wizard's head screaming, "Aaaahhhh!"

Kerlith quickly flashed his stone up high and called out, "Apokrothos," repelling the ghoul into the air and away from them.

"Nice," Bel said but perspiration was heavy on his brow.

The four squeezed in, pushing their backs against each other and slowly rotating, knowing now that the attack could come from any direction.

Bel tried to focus his eyes on any incoming threat but he couldn't get the smell of decaying vegetation and sloppy wet mud out of his mind. It invaded his nostrils the moment they arrived and it wouldn't leave. Some smells you get used to if you are around them long enough. This wasn't one of them. There was something primeval and base about the dank mud they were treading in. Bel morbidly thought, Is this where I am to die? In this mud?

A larger group of them was gathering on the other side of the short street in the center of the village and it appeared one was addressing the crowd.

"A leader. Look. They have a leader," Nes'egrinon whispered and dread seeped into Bel's skin. The next onslaught would be coordinated.

The leader turned and walked slowly and alone towards the mages, them waiting, watching, not knowing if this might be a distraction or a ploy. A ghoul jumped out from between two building and the old wizard quickly flung him into the woods with a wave of his staff. Another ran by and oil splashed down on his head and a youngster, not yet a teenager threw a torch on him.

The gray skinned leader stopped about ten paces from them, slurped some blood out of a flask then opened his voice wide. "You can't win, you know."

He waited for a response but when none came he continued, "We ghoul-kind don't need to sleep. We can keep up at this all night. And tomorrow. And the next day." He was speaking loudly; loud enough so all the villagers could hear him. It was a mental barrage, psychology, and the worst volley of all to defend against.

Bel overheard a woman on the second floor say, "Oh my God. It's the Mayor."

The dead man took another draught of blood, then said, "You all just don't understand! We wouldn't do this if we didn't have to! It's the hunger. The thirst for life. Nothing can stand against it. Not patience, not fear, not superstitious beliefs. No, not even disgust. Do not think that you are better than us for when it comes upon you,

you will abandon everything to satiate this lingering starvation. I know. I have fought it with all my strength and I have failed. This is torment! And you have within you the ability to take it away! Even if just for a moment. A few drops of blood. Please! You can stop this! Just a few drops of blood from each of you."

The mayor turned, all eyes on him, and joined his group at the end of the street. They waited for some moments, glancing at each other wildly, expectantly, hooting shrilly as if they were wild dogs about to be fed.

What he said didn't matter; everyone knew it was all a lie. There wasn't enough blood in all the living to satisfy all the dead. And what about when it wore off? They would want more. And more. And more.

They charged, a stampeding army, sordid, savage, beating their chests, the thought of blood only moments away driving a wild glaze into their eyes. Villagers desperately filled buckets with oil as the blitz closed in while others ran somewhere, anywhere, to hide. But everyone knew there was nowhere to hide. Not from them.

There must be something we can do to scare them off that does not involve letting them get too close. Bel thought on this as the group of dead quickly approached. Fear, Bel thought. Back at Lasaat, we used Fear on each other in our mock mage battles. Bel remembered those days fondly. Fear. Yes, that's it. That's what the Mayor said too. If only there were something like Fear that we could push into the ghoul-kind. Then it came to him. Bel raised both of his hands, his staff high in the air and pushed out as he said the words in the ancient language, "Eros!"

Suddenly the group of approaching ghoul-kind wailed out in fear, terror on every one of their faces. They ran into the forest howling in panic. Bel smiled. He was shocked that it actually worked.

Kerlith said, "What did you do?" as his master and Nes'egrinon stood nearby.

Bel answered, "What is the opposite of fear, but love? An old love spell, only good for barmaids trying to catch her a sailor probably. That's what I used. I figured it would —"

The old wizard interrupted, "See, I told you. He's not as dumb as he looks. That's why I picked him. Still talks too much though."

"Shall we then?" Muolithnon said gruffly.

The four joined hands. Nes'egrinon raised up their arms and cried out, "Focus. Focus. Not yet. Concentrate. Focus it. Wait for it. Okay. Okay. Now!"

They released a sudden burst of power, concentrated in the form of the love spell and a ripple erupted and washed out of them and outward, outward, outward, a light purple, misty cloud carrying a strong scent of jasmine out and over both the people and ghoul-kind alike, extending out into the forest. They released their hands and let their arms fall, exhausted. Muolithnon slumped his chin into his chest and heaved. Bel felt like he might collapse but was suddenly jolted upright by the high-pitched shrieks of the dead. They scrambled and ran as fast as they could in an unorganized chaotic jumble of gray limbs fighting each other to be the first ones out of the town. They scrambled this way and that, seemingly not knowing which way led to an escape. The four stood and watched as ghoul-kind fell from second floor balconies and clamored from under porches and behind barns. They had been lying in wait everywhere! They fled.

The old mage said softly, "Keep your mouths shut and follow my lead." He walked back towards the inn.

People were gathering themselves and their belongs, men helping women, women helping men, softly, kindly, with a smile, a nod, a caress and a gesture. As they neared the entrance to the inn several women appeared near the door, smiles wide and beaming.

"No need to thank us, ladies. Just another day on the job for a wizard of the wood," the old mage said.

"Oh no. We really need to thank you. Really we do. Really, really we do. How about a massage?" one said.

Another said, "How about a manicure? A pedicure? I can draw you a bath? Anything. Ask anything. Please. Please. Ask, please."

Two younger ones swooped around the two mages and stood on either side of Kerlith and Bel. One said, "We would really, really like to thank your young assistants. It wouldn't be right for us not to."

The other added, "Yes, yes, yes. It is our custom. We mustn't be rude. Please come with us. Come with us, right away." The two girls grabbed the boys' arms and began to tug.

Other girls arrived and pushed the first group of girls back. "Hey, we need to thank them too."

"Me first."

"No! Me!"

Nes'egrinon bellowed, "Quiet! That's what I was afraid of. Like a cackling bunch of hens. That's exactly what I don't need now. Women!"

Muolithnon interrupted, "Err, Master Archmage? Are you sure? I wouldn't mind being thanked just a little."

"Yeah!" Harped from the women. "See! See! He wants to be thanked."

"I saw him first!"

"Get away! He's mine!"

The old man threw his hands in the air and replied, "Do what you want just don't wake me up. Fifth Year let's go. You'll thank me in the morning for saving you from *these*."

Bel was not so sure about that last statement but he followed his master into the inn, up the stairs and back into his bed. But there would be no sleep for him this night. He had too much to dwell on.

Chapter Eight

Bite Me

"Love magic. Making love magic. I love some love making magic."

"Is he going to be like that all morning?" Bel asked Kerlith.

Kerlith shrugged his shoulders as his master danced around their room.

Nes'egrinon said, "It's about time we move on from this place. We can steal away while the ghoul-kind are asleep in the forest and the village folk should have at least a few days respite after what happened last night. Fifth Year, by the way, I didn't get a chance to compliment you."

Bel and Kerlith both turned their attention to the old mage.

He looked up and them and squinted. "Oh, why are

you two staring at me?"

Bel replied, "A compliment? You said something about a compliment?"

"I said I didn't get a chance to give you one. I didn't say I was planning on doing it, did I? Well anyway, good job. Now let's get this place packed up and ready. We're leaving shortly."

Muolithnon interrupted, "Master Archmage, the villagers, they would really like us to stay. At least one more day. You know I don't get away from the stonecutters too much and these fair maidens in your wood have taken a liking… I mean, it would be better if we stayed one more day, just to make sure that the ghouls really got the message. Don't you think?"

"I don't think. This was all your idea. You're the one who dragged me out here. But if we stay here too long I just might head back home. No need for me to stick around while you cast love spells. That's for sure. Listen, what's your problem anyway? Can't get a date amongst the stonecutters, huh? You must be uglier than I thought. And what about the ban? You took the vow didn't you?"

Muolithnon replied, "Err… I think one more night should send the message to the ghoul-kind. We can do as before. Wait for them to mass upon us and join forces and cast a great love spell. Maybe even a bigger one this time. I have my jacket out at the washroom. It's getting cleaned just for the occasion and I have an appointment at the barber. A shave and a haircut… oh, no! I'm late. Darn this eternal night! Never know what time it is! I'm off. Kerlith, heed the master while I'm gone. I won't be long." He quickly exited with a wide grin and there was almost a twinkle in his eye.

Bel asked, "Master, shall I have breakfast prepared for you?"

"After that display! No. My stomach is twisting. You two go ahead. I need some time alone to think."

Bel and Kerlith ate then sat out on the front porch watching the villagers attempting to conduct their daily business by torchlight, them behaving as if the events of last night did not happen, as if they weren't nearly all slaughtered.

They are a tough people. Resilient, Bel thought. Their village sat right on the border between the Hinterlands and the Western Forest and they had been right on the dividing line of the war. It was a long war and a long time ago but the name of this village appeared in all the histories. They saw fighting, too much fighting, outside forces invading, retreating and invading again, trying to capture a strategic position without care or concern for the people who lived here. No, these ghoul attacks must be bringing those memories back like a dam breaking and pouring in a carcass-laden fetid stream of death, Bel thought.

"I guess life goes on?" Bel said trying to clear his

mind.

"I was thinking the same thing, but maybe it's just because they have no other choice. They can't run. They can't hide. I guess the best they can do is pretend it didn't happen. I mean the alternative would be to run around in the center courtyard here like a babbling, insane person. I mean, like if you really sat down and thought about it."

"Hey, is your master always like that?"

"I don't know. Is yours?" Kerlith snapped back.

"No, I didn't mean it like that. I meant… I don't know what I meant. He took advantage of those girls, you know."

"Looked like they were taking advantage of him."

"Maybe. But still, they were under a spell. I don't care what you two do as long as you don't mess things up for us in the forest. This is our lands remember?"

"Maybe that was just an excuse they used to let their hair down a little. Maybe they wanted to do that all along. I see your master wasn't interested. What's his malfunction?"

"He's old, I guess," Bel defended.

"That has nothing to do with it."

"And he wouldn't let you out either. Maybe he was afraid you'd embarrass him."

"Really, Kerlith? And how'd you do?"

"I did all right. You won't find any young girls complaining this morning. I'm a regular all around fun person to be with, I am."

"Oh. Yeah. I knew that. Barrel of monkeys, you are."

Kerlith huffed as he threw a pebble, "You got that right."

Bel's heart suddenly ached over leaving the only girl he ever loved to become a wizard (of course, all magicians were required to take an oath of celibacy) and the knowledge that he would never see her again gnawed his flesh. Shireen. He missed her desperately. The only thing he knew to do was to push the thought of her out of his mind.

He couldn't understand how Kerlith and his master flaunted the rules so casually. He couldn't understand why he had to leave the girl he wanted to spend his life with while these two could go out cavorting whenever they pleased. "But what if you got caught? Aren't you worried about the ban?"

Kerlith eyed Bel quickly then looked back at the courtyard. "My master doesn't seem to be. Why should I?"

"I don't know. I was kind of glad when my master pulled me upstairs."

"Yeah, I was in the game; you were tucked in your bed like the child you are."

Bel bristled but before he could respond, a young boy that stood in front of the two wizards in training interrupted them, "Masters? Sirs? Might I ask a question, sirs?"

Kerlith replied first, "Sure kid, what are you looking for? An autograph or something?"

"No, sir. I was wondering if you could tell me something about magic. We don't get many wizards in these parts. And when we do they tend to be old. One day, I would be a wizard. At least that is my dream."

Kerlith puffed out his chest. "Sure thing. See this kid sitting next to me? You can call him wiggle-farts. So wiggle-farts and I went to Lasaat. Ever heard of it?"

Bel's forehead was burning bright red. Wiggle-farts was a nickname he got in his first year. One of the others saw him shake once when he had gas and the rest was history. He hated that name; he thought it might disappear when he left Lasaat but now Kerlith was perpetuating it.

"Yes sir. The University of Arts and Magic?"

"That's the one. You have to be selected to go. Don't know how exactly it works, but they can see something in you. The scouts, I mean. Some are found when they are ten or eleven, others are not found until they are older, even as old as sixteen or seventeen."

A falcon landed on the building edge, its feet grasping the gutter edge tightly, and looked down at them with a glint in its eye.

Bel added, "Oh, I remember that day like it was yesterday. They showed up in my tiny fishing village and made a beeline for my house. Caused a great stir, they did.

All the villagers followed them, wanting to know who the strangers were looking for. By their dress everyone knew exactly who they were. You know the ones, right?"

"Yes, sir," answered the boy.

"It was quite a shock for my parents, of course. What with my father expecting me to join him on the waters. He was a fisherman, you see."

Kerlith interrupted, "Yeah, me too. I was only twelve and here these two men were, asking me to leave everything, to never see my family again, my parents, my brothers and sisters and my kin, to never return to my village, to never see my people again. I cried for two nights. I'm not embarrassed to say it. Yeah, I cried. I was just a kid, understand? Don't laugh or I'll smash you. But yeah, it was a lot for a little kid to take in. The rest of the village wanted me to go because they thought I would be coming back after the schooling to be their wizard, to protect them. But no, that's not how it works. I haven't seen my family since."

"I see," said the young boy. "And the school, is it hard?"

Kerlith smiled wide and said, "Kid, most people take five years to graduate—"

Bel pounced, "Shut it, Kerlith. Shut it before—"

"Before what? Before you get mad? Oh, I'm getting real, real scared, I am. I'm like shaking all over. Oh, I hope a fart doesn't come out. Oh, I'm wiggling, I am."

"Jerk! I took six years only because of you! It was all your fault I got left back!"

"Really? It was you who took the challenge. You didn't have to. You could have kept your big mouth shut. But no! You had to look like the big man in front of the others. And it was your spell that blew up in your face anyway!"

Bel wanted to respond but he knew it was true. Sometimes Bel couldn't stand Kerlith and his mouth and his arrogant, in-your-face attitude. It was stupid of Bel to respond to him; he knew it, but Kerlith caught him on a bad day. School was tough; there had been a few difficult tests and one of Bel's friends dropped out. So when Kerlith started another one of his verbal barrages, Bel lost it. Before he knew it he had agreed to a challenge, off the grounds, at midnight, away from the eyes of the masters. It was forbidden. They battled long and hard, all of their friends watching, each spell more complicated, more delicate, more risky. Finally Bel did something he hadn't done before. He used stone magic. It shouldn't have worked. He was holding mage-wood in his hand; he shouldn't have been able to wield the words of crystal. But it worked. And then he lost control of it. The others ran for help. It took four masters to subdue the magic run amok. No one was hurt, but the damage was done. He wasn't kicked out of the school, thankfully, but he was not permitted to graduate for another year.

Bel sat in silence watching as the large hawk mounted

the wind. Kerlith asked the lad, "Okay, kid. Any other questions? Looks like wiggle-farts here doesn't want to talk about school."

"Yes, sir. If you please? I noticed that you use a stone while he uses a stick? Why is that?"

"You want to take this one?" Kerlith said with a smirk.

"You go ahead. Idiot."

"Kid, it's like this. There are different forms of magic. In school we were all taught the common stuff, the magic that any magician can do, but there are other forms that are specific, different forms that only specialized wizards can do. There is one form based upon crystals and minerals, from the mountain lands, the land of the stonecutters. We call it stone magic. There is a magic of the desert-lands and one of the tundra-lands. Another is based upon plant life, like trees and such, from the forest-lands. That's the form that the kid here is learning. In the end they are all the same in one way. The source of all power is life. Everyone knows this. Magic is merely a manipulation of the life-force in all of us and in all living things."

"But rocks are not living," the young boy stated.

Nes'egrinon interrupted, "Well said, young man. Well said." Bel and Kerlith quickly turned their heads back to the master. Neither knew he was there listening. The mage continued, "Myself, I cannot understand this magic of rocks and crystals. It makes no sense to me. How could it work? There is no life in rock. How can a wizard call forth power from it? It's dead. Baah. Makes no sense."

Kerlith replied, "Master, certainly you know that crystal, while not alive, can act as a sort of prism, bending the light that is already in the world, focusing it, concentrating it into a pinpoint."

"Yes, of course I knew that. But it would be much easier to just go to the source of life instead of bending it, don't you think? Here feel this." The old wizard held out his staff. "This staff was cut from a one thousand year old mage-wood tree that still stands today. That tree's roots go long and deep, thousands of feet down into the ground. I wouldn't be surprised if all mage-wood trees were not part of the same one tree; its roots go out so far. And this staff, this piece of wood, still contains the form of life of that tree, the body that was full of light, the casing, if you will. The great wizard Lucretius called them atoms and said that they are in all of us and in all things living. Can you feel it? Can you feel the power? I don't have to search for light to bend and focus. This mage-wood, this casing in my hand is the natural home of light; it feels comfortable there. It wants to be there. When I call for light with mage-wood in my hand it comes readily, even eagerly. But a stone? Light does not belong there. It must be coaxed, forced even. Baah, it makes no sense."

The young boy wandered off so Bel said, "Master? At

Lasaat, Rylithnon said that someday a mage would come who would unite all magic. He said it was foretold. A mage who could harness all of the nine forms, both living and non-living, both of the creature and of the land."

"Ridiculous. Hogwash. He said that? Foolishness." The old mage leaned against the back wall of the building, shaking his head and looking at the floor.

Kerlith continued, "I think it was kind of like his personal conquest. Even though he was called to stone magic, he wanted to learn everything about all of the nine forms. He constantly spoke to the other masters about it."

"What? And he spoke openly of this?"

Bel replied, "Yes, Master. Err... not to say what I did wasn't wrong. It was. I know that now. But sometimes I think that was why he held me back. Because a student of forest magic somehow was able to speak the magic of life from the book of stone mages. Even though it went terribly wrong."

"Well, of course it did! It's not in your nature. It is absolutely, positively unnatural! What were you thinking, boy?"

"I don't know. Seemed like a good idea at the time."

"Really? Well don't have any such good ideas when you're out with me. Just do what you're told. If you decide you're going to do something you haven't been taught then don't. A forest-mage doing stone magic, huh! Insane!"

The old mage walked back behind the building

leaving Kerlith and Bel in silence.

Muolithnon sang as he walked up to them, grabbing Bel and Kerlith's attention, "Now check out this shave! Oh yeah! I'm a clean, slippery fish. Can't wait for tonight. Apprentice, feel how clean my neck is."

"I'd rather not," Kerlith replied.

"C'mon, c'mon, feel it. Right there, right there. Feel how smooth it is." The mage leaned in closer and tilted his head back.

"Errr... okay?" Kerlith touched his master's neck and the mage squealed, "Did you feel that? Nice and smooth. Yes, sir! Here, Fifth Year, ahh, Bel, feel my neck?"

"No thanks. I need to check on my master." Bel hopped up and ducked into the inn.

Bel scaled the staircase, entered their room and busied himself with putting his meager belongings into his sack. A long dark shadow formed near the window as a hawk flapped its wings on the other side of the glass. Bel walked towards it and saw Master Nes'egrinon standing there in the shadows, or at least he seemed to standing there. Or floating. It was hard to be certain in the dim light. The youth blinked his eyes and there he was. The mage stood motionless. Bel knew what he thought he saw, what he thought had happened, and he was in awe. Could it be that his master was the same hawk that watched them out in the front of the building some minutes ago? Bel had heard legends of wizards of old being able to transform themselves into such creatures but he, like almost everyone, thought the legends were false and impossible. No one could do that. He stared at him, their eyes met and Bel realized that he truly was the greatest wizard in all of the known lands. Bel looked away; he could not hold the archmage's gaze. There was nothing mean or condescending in his dark eyes yet there was something there that made Bel feel small and the rest of the world very large, the world that Bel did not know and had only heard rumor of, something there, in those eyes, that had seen too much, a vast land of power and intrigue, war and pain, love and loss, and it made Bel feel insignificant and very, very tiny. He did not fear his eyes but he could not stare into the infinity in them either.

The wizard stepped out from the dark and said, "Fifth Year, tell me what will happen tonight."

Bel shook away his thoughts. "Tonight? I am not a seer. I—"

"If you had been a seer then I would not have chosen you. I am not asking you if you have seen the future only tell me what you think will happen."

"I think much like yesterday. Except, I suppose, the ghoul-kind know of this new defense we have so… so they will not come at us in the same way," Bel replied.

"Go on."

"Last night they did not fear us so they rallied a full frontal attack assuming that the town would quickly crumble. Now they know that we are here so, perhaps, they will try to take us out first? But they know a mass of ghouls rushing us will not work. Perhaps they will try to sneak in?"

The master rubbed his chin. "Yes, I think you are right. That is what I would do if I were leading them."

"And we know something else. That they have a leader. At least one leader, anyway. There may be more."

"Good. Good. Think on this more. We will leave soon, perhaps in the morning, perhaps sooner. Be watchful. Be waiting. Do not let your guard down. And store."

"Store?" The teen asked.

"Yes. Collect energy. Gather it; call to it. There is light. It is far off, but do not be fooled; there is still light in the lands. Call for it now, while it is day, at least daytime somewhere, and gather the light. Store it. We will need it if they attack."

"Yes, Master."

"And one other thing, don't let that stone apprentice get under your skin. I don't need you distracted out there."

"Don't worry. He won't."

Bel told Kerlith what his master had said so they spent the rest of the evening out near the rear of the blacksmith's shed, away from prying eyes, gathering light. The tiny filaments streamed in, some through the sky and coming from distant lands, others from within the village.

Some children took to following the wisps of light around and tracked them to where the two sat, eyes clenched, minds locked in a deep concentration. After a time Bel felt more full of energy than he had ever felt. It was an odd sensation.

"Never done this before, huh?" Kerlith quizzed.

"No. You?"

"Never. Never had to. We were always surrounded by life. Who needed to store it up when it was always so plentiful?"

Bel stood and arched his back and looked down at his hands. They looked swollen, as if something inside was pushing to get out and it still bothered him that some of this energy, this life-force that he now held inside of him, most likely came from the villagers. Indeed, even these small children running around him at his knees bothered him as they cried out, "More lights! Make the funny lights come back! Please!" Though Bel knew they were using it to protect them, something didn't quite feel right about taking it without asking.

Kerlith broke Bel's thoughts. "It is near time. Let's go back to the front. The others must be preparing."

They walked from behind the buildings to see Muolithnon standing in the center court addressing the people. "It won't be long, my dear people. We will scatter the ghoul-kind then we will be off to stop this eternal night. Mark my words, I am a mage and do not lie."

Many of the people on the second floor clapped, especially the women, while the men grunted and filled the barrels with oil. Bel and Kerlith joined him and soon Nes'egrinon slowly hobbled out to accompany them.

"Phew. What's that rank smell?" the aged wizard asked incredulously.

Muolithnon replied, "What... I beg your pardon. That's my perfume."

"Oh that will do nicely. We'll stink the dead away. What'd you do that for? How are we supposed to travel unnoticed in the forest with you smelling like a barrel of rotten cheese?"

The magician turned and waved to a group of women on a far balcony then replied, "I think the scent is quite nice. It's not for you anyway."

Kerlith interrupted, "There. The dead. They're coming."

The others looked where he was pointing, at the far end of the forest, barely visible from their location. A horde of dead scrambled through the trees at the edge of the forest, their clothing draped from them shredded and soiled with dirt and dry-caked blood. They moved in a panicked aggression, nearly a stampede, as if they could barely control the urge to run, the blood lust was so strong.

"Yes, looks like they are trying to outflank us. They're going to follow behind that row of buildings then that would put them about there." The wizard said, perfume wafting off his arm as he pointed between two adjacent buildings about fifteen paces away. "That will still give us enough time to prepare. There is no way they can get from that opening to here without us seeing them."

Kerlith said, "Master, when are we going to do the big spell?"

Muolithnon replied, "As much as I'd like to just let it fly right now, it would be much better if we didn't have to do it at all. It requires a huge amount of energy and it would be nice if we could stay fresh for our journey. Besides, maybe the ghouls have wizened up and won't attack at all. We'll see."

Then they charged; ghouls came running out from the adjacent buildings and it was so sudden that even though the wizards knew they would attack, it caught them off guard. It was a concerted attack, but like Nes'egrinon and Bel had discussed, different than before.

"Apokrothos!" Bel howled as light flashed from the tip of his staff, sending two ghouls sailing far and disappearing into the cold night air. Another ran out and another. Each time one of the mages sent the dead person flying far into the woods. But each time they got just a bit closer. Wave after wave of ghoul-kind streamed in never leaving a gap of more than a few seconds between them. The last one's hand touched on Muolithnon's sleeve just as he sent him flying. The dead man's odor was still in

Muolithnon's nostrils as he rubbed his wrist where the ghoul grabbed him and he muttered, "We should send out the spell."

"Yes, prepare yourselves," Nes'egrinon replied.

Ghouls had somehow gained a foothold in two of the buildings on either side of the center court and were massed on the first floors. They ran out in pairs from each building synchronously, flailing their arms and screaming, charging at them from either side. The smell was hideous, the rank decay of rotting flesh.

Nes'egrinon slammed his staff into the ground sending out a tremor that knocked both ghoul-kind and human-kind to the ground. But the dead quickly bound to their feet and continued the attack. Their eyes were glazed. They wanted blood and wanted it now.

The wizards and their apprentices alternately took turns motioning with their staffs or stones flinging the corpses into the air and away from them; the wizards somehow trying to create a gap in the action so they could organize the love spell but stopping the onslaught, even for a moment, was proving nearly impossible. Windows on the buildings smashed as chairs flew through and more ghouls exited through the first floor windows. Now they were coming at them four or five at a time. Each time they flung the ghouls away, the creatures crashed into buildings or the muddy ground, then stood, shook themselves and straightened out their broken limbs, then returned to the fight. There was no stopping them.

The people on the second floor were pouring oil onto the ghouls below but then the dead reached the landing and pushed people off the balconies or dragged them back inside screaming, kicking, clawing and fighting. Once the dead gained control of the two balconies, one leapt off of it towards them, then another, then another. Bel looked over at Kerlith, a worrisome look in his eyes, as the two began to wonder when they were going to repel the whole lot of them with the love spell.

Bel wiped his forehead, thinking it might be starting to rain, then realized that it was the slathering spittle of falling ghoul-kind.

Nes'egrinon said, "It is time. We need to do this now. They are getting too close," while he continued to fling away ghoul after ghoul after ghoul.

"Aye," Muolithnon said with a smile. Then a ghoul landed on him.

"Apokrothos!" Kerlith screamed as he clenched his mage-stone and swung his arm in a broad stroke sending the dead man on a tall arc deep into the woods.

Bel and his master closed ranks as Kerlith bent over his fallen teacher. "Master! Are you okay?" But even as he spoke Kerlith knew that everything was not okay. Blood poured on the side of Muolithnon's head and as Kerlith turned it, he saw that part of his master's ear was missing. It had been bitten off.

Kerlith stood. "Now! We must do it now! The three of us, so I can attend to my master!"

Nes'egrinon looked down at the puddle of blood forming around the wizard's head and said, "Yes. But breathe for a moment first. It will do no good to release it in anger. It is a love spell after all. Calm yourself. Okay? Okay? Join hands. Gather your minds."

While Bel and Kerlith closed their eyes and focused, the old master continued to fling away incoming attackers, barely able to keep them away by himself. "Okay, now bring it up. Raise your hands. Bring it up to a crescendo. When you can't hold it anymore, release it."

The pressure built higher and higher and Bel felt as if in each moment he couldn't hold it for one second longer. But he did. He had no idea how he did it but he did. He held onto it even though the pressure was going to blow him apart.

Then Kerlith howled, "Now!" and they both pushed with all their might, expelling it, giving birth, bringing forth life; it burst out of them in a resounding shockwave. A purple, hazy cloud erupted around them and wafted across the village and out into the woods and the ghoul-kind ran in a frenzied panic back into the forest.

Kerlith bent over his master and pushed healing into him, hard.

A grave look on his face, Nes'egrinon placed his hand on the apprentice's shoulder and said, "Hold, son. Not too much. Be careful now. You don't want to drain yourself. Not here. Let's get him into the inn."

They scooped him up and carried him inside, placing him on one of the dining tables. The room filled with women cooing, some asking if they could help. The frail wizard slammed his staff down hard onto the floorboards, howling, "Out!" A shockwave knocked plates off the walls and cracked plaster and floorboards around them. The women scattered.

The mage placed his hand over the young wizards ear and the two teens placed their hands on Nes'egrinon's back, feeding their life-energy into him. After a number of moments, the old wizard removed his hand and the wound was sealed, but it had a grayness to it.

"Master, the poison of the dead? How do we stop it?" Kerlith asked, his voice near cracking.

"I do not know," Nes'egrinon replied as he slumped into a chair and daze painted over his face.

Chapter Nine

Then There Were Three

"How's he doing?" Bel asked Kerlith, trying to mask what he was thinking, the grim inevitability that his master would soon be dead.

"Doing? How do you think he's doing? Look at him. His skin continues to become more and more gray. It's almost all gray now, head to foot. He already looks dead. I don't know how he's holding on to tell you the truth. And, well, he stinks."

"I know. The smell's everywhere. Decay?"

Kerlith threw his hands up and clenched down his eyes. "He's rotting."

"Hey, calm down. How about you? You don't look too good either."

"Well, how good could I be? Here I am stuck in the middle of the woods. Me, an apprentice to a stone-mage. You know our magic isn't that strong when we get away from our lands. We shouldn't even be here. And here he lies. Look at him. My master. And what's to become of me? If he dies, I'm too far along in my training to find another to teach me. Who would take me? Especially after this. There aren't enough masters for new apprentices as it is. And if I become a second, then what? I'll be stuck hauling water and pig feed for another year? And I'm not far enough on to try to take the tests."

"But you have to go on. You have to complete the training. You don't want to become a second-class village magician, do you?"

"What choice do I have?"

Bel's voice felt shallow as he stared at the man dying. "I don't know. What's it been? Three days?"

Kerlith leapt up and walked to the window and looked out at the street below. "Days? Huh. Hadn't thought... I guess. It's so hard to tell without sunlight, isn't it? I was watching the villagers and how they light the torches brighter during the day—what we call day, anyway —then I got to wondering. How do they know?"

"The ghouls? The ghoul-kind only attack at night."

"But since this happened," Kerlith waved his hand at

Muolithnon lying on the bed. "Since this happened they haven't been attacking much at all. And I've been watching them. Sometimes they send in a few during what we think is daytime. I don't know anymore. I'm not sure what is day or night."

"You think they're planning something big?"

"No, I think they're waiting for something." Kerlith turned away from the window and looked back at the mage on the bed. "I think they're waiting for him."

"Eeeeaaaarrrr!" Muolithnon squeaked out then gasped hard, eyes wide and back arched.

Kerlith bolted to his side, "Master, I'm here."

"Bee bo bee billlber bo be," Muolithnon babbled then closed his eyes.

Kerlith slumped back into the chair next to the bed. "Gibberish. Gibberish, again."

"Maybe someone will come? My master sent out a sending. Hopefully one of the other masters will come. Maybe one from the Tundra-lands. They are supposed to be most adept at healing injuries."

Kerlith looked up at Bel and said what they both already knew, "From this there is no healing."

Nes'egrinon entered their room. "Phew! It stinks in here! Open a window!"

"Yes, master," Bel said and quickly did as he requested.

The old mage pinched his nose shut and said, "How

can you two sit in that? Okay listen. I sent out a sending, just so you know, but… no one is coming. The darkness has spread to the desert and as far as the mountains in the east. We know that much anyway. Back west, in Lasaat, there is no darkness yet. But, I don't know, something is wrong there. I spoke with Jergamemnon. It appears that Rylithnon has been gone for some time. And some others. It's not exactly clear but it appears that they went out, as we have, to discover the source of this eternal darkness."

Bel couldn't hide his smile. "So that's good. There are others out trying to fight this. Perhaps we will meet them on our way?"

"Problem is they haven't replied to the sending. None of them."

Kerlith asked, "What does that mean?"

"I don't know. Perhaps when a person comes too close to the breach or enters into it then the sending will not work. Certainly no one can send into the land of the dead. It is forbidden. And maybe not even possible. But with the breach open… I do not know."

No one wanted to say the obvious—that they could all be dead. No one wanted to say it because if a handful of masters from Lasaat, their teachers, the ones chosen from among all the masters to teach were dead, then what chance did a wizard long past his years and two newly appointed apprentices have? The room grew quiet.

"Eeeeaaaarrrr!" Muolithnon squealed as his hand

unconsciously groped at his side for something.

Nes'egrinon's shoulders tensed and after the man on his deathbed stopped squirming the mage motioned for Kerlith to step out into the hall. Bel followed him to hear what he would say. "Listen, I need you to remove all of your master's stones. All of them. Rings, necklaces, anything with any magical properties that he could use. Okay?"

Kerlith face contorted uncomfortably because he knew exactly why he was being asked to do this. In case they had to fight him after he died. "But. I can't."

"You have to. You don't have any choice. Fifth Year, you help him. Make sure it happens. We don't need this situation becoming any worse."

"Yes, Master," Bel replied, not trying to sound too eager in front of Kerlith.

"Good. I'll be in the back trying another sending. Come tell me when it is done. Bring me everything."

"And Master?" Bel glanced at Kerlith and back to the mage then said, "The villagers, they've been talking. They think we should send him out into the forest now. I was just wondering. What are we going to do? When he dies?"

"I've been thinking on that. It's a hard one. If we send him out into the forest then we may have to fight him later. And then how could we leave? I would feel responsible. We couldn't. But what else can we do? We can't keep him inside with us here. The villagers wouldn't stand for it. And they probably shouldn't. So I was thinking, when he dies, we leave and we take him with us."

"What?" Kerlith yelped.

"I know. It's a risk."

Bel asked, "But we are heading into the mountains?"

The wizard looked at Bel. "It seems so. I know. The land of stone and rock. He should become stronger while I will become weaker when we leave the forest. But what choice do we have?" He lowered his voice to a whisper. "If we leave him here this village will fall in minutes. I cannot do that to my people."

Kerlith tried to turn the conversation. "Do you expect him to help us after he is dead?"

Nes'egrinon's voice suddenly sounded haggard. "I don't know. I think so. I hope. Just because he's dead doesn't mean he turns into a monster. He will be the same person, just dead."

Kerlith's face brightened then frowned. "But the thirst, Master Nes'egrinon? What shall we do about the thirst?"

Suddenly the old man looked angry. "Does it look like I have all this planned out? You kids again. You think I've got all the answers. I don't. I don't. Can't you see that? You're not in school anymore. This is not a lesson plan. This is real. Okay? One step at a time. We leave. We take him. I don't know. Hopefully find some small animals along the way that can keep him satiated. I don't know. We find this *so called* breach. Where? I don't know. But say we find it. Then what? I don't know. We do something about it. Hopefully we can close it. I don't know. Maybe. If not, we call the others. Get some help. What's the alternative here?"

The two said nothing so Nes'egrinon turned and left.

Removing Muolithnon's stones was less difficult than they imagined. The mage was mostly unconscious and didn't know what they were doing. After he pulled off his master's last stone, a large polished ring made from jade, Kerlith said, "It won't be long now. Without these he will die faster."

"I can take them to my master if you want to stay with him."

Kerlith passed Bel the stones, all except one, the ring. He put it on his own finger.

Bel left the room and scampered down the stairs. All eyes in the inn were on him and all conversations stopped. As he traversed the hall one man standing at the counter yelled out, "It stinks in here!"

Bel tightened up his shoulders and paused, then continued walking.

"Hey! I'm talking to you, kid!"

The boy stopped at the door and turned to look back at the man.

"You can't keep a dead man up there. Wizard or no.

We don't want no dead here. Got it," the man hissed his words.

Bel couldn't read the crowd, but none of them dissented. He replied, "We will take him out as soon as he dies."

"What are you waiting for? He ain't gonna make it. No one does. He's as good as dead now. Tell you what. I'll help you carry him out right now."

Nes'egrinon stepped inside. "That won't be necessary." Bel was relieved to see him. He had no idea what to say to the man. The wizard said to Bel, "Come. Pack your things. We leave now."

Bel passed his master the stones. The two scaled the steps and opened the door to their room to find Muolithnon sitting upright. Bel caught his breath for a moment as the thought that the wizard was somehow miraculously cured left him and he realized that he was dead. He was a ghoul.

Nes'egrinon walked in the room and stood in front of the dead man. He spoke softly. "Old friend. We must leave now. You are coming with us."

"Yes. I... I feel odd."

"Come. We must go now." He looked at both of the young boys and nodded.

They quickly gathered up their belongings. Kerlith pulled his master's hood over his head and pulled it down to obscure his face then grabbed his elbow and tugged.

"This way. Come. Come. Let's go." The newly dead man was disoriented but he followed the apprentice out of the room and down the stairs.

Nes'egrinon kept them moving quickly and clearly wanted to make a fast exit to avoid any protests from the villagers. He handed the barman some coins and said, "Here you are, my good man. This should more than cover our stay."

As the four walked out a woman at the tables yelled out, "You're not leaving, are you?"

They kept walking but Bel became nervous when he heard the legs of a few chairs scrape the wood plank floor. People were standing up. He refused to look over at them.

Another called out, "You can't! You can't leave us! We're surrounded! The ghoul-kind!"

Two men stood and blocked the exit just as they reached the doors. Others began yelling out, begging them to stay. The wizard looked deeply into the men's eyes and said, "Son, you don't want to do that." The man's face melted, knowing there was no way he could stop the wizard, then he moved from their path.

The four walked out of the inn then quickly ducked behind the building and grabbed torches. Kerlith and Bel filled both their water and oil flasks then they followed the old man into the woods on a narrow winding path. Ten paces in, the woods became so dense that it felt as if they could be miles if not hundreds of miles from civilization.

As they walked Bel forced his mind to other things to avoid the idea that what they were doing was madness. All madness. His mind wandered to the thought of fishing on the water with his father. It was a simple time. He would sit on the bow, bouncing with the waves, calling out for school-sign. Where there were schools of small fish, there were always larger fish, predators, hunting near the large groups. When he saw them, he would call out and his father would heave to and anchor. Bel's memories were flushed when the dead man spoke. "What? Where?"

The wizard replied, "Keep walking, my old friend. All will become clear."

A few ghouls met them on the path but none of the marauder type so they did not contest but moved out of the way and let them pass. The dead people all recognized them from before and knew what they could do. A few asked for blood but did nothing when the mage-kind did not respond but merely continued on.

The newly dead man did not walk as fast as the others; he lumbered, almost zombie-like. It wasn't that his leg was injured or anything like that, but he somehow didn't have the motivation to do it, like he was a small child who was following his mother but really didn't want to.

They walked on the path for a long time. It rose and fell, twisted and turned and occasionally broke into clearings. If the clearing was elevated then they might be able to see to the horizon. If not and they wanted to check their bearings then someone had to climb a tree. The path didn't have many forks so the two young men only had to each climb once as yet. At first Bel wasn't even so sure that they were heading the right way, and maybe he was kind of okay with that, but as it got colder he knew they were heading into the mountains.

The group stopped when they came to a small bridge over a stream. They all drank deeply and filled their flasks, all except the dead man.

Muolithnon was becoming more coherent. "I am dead, aren't I? I feel strange." He stared at his gray arms in his gray jacket. "I didn't think it would feel like this. My mind's kind of foggy. I'm hungry too."

The three started at that last sentence.

"Oh. Hahaha. Don't worry. I'm not going to bite you. Hahaha. I'll just call a rabbit. Hey where's my ring? And... Hey, where's my stone?" He was perturbed.

Nes'egrinon stood up from the soft earth he was sitting on. "Don't worry. We have them. We didn't know what to do. You would have removed them if it were one of us."

"Aye. I would have." He calmed down. "Well, let me have them then. I'm getting hungry."

"I don't know if—"

The dead man grew angry and cut his words. "You don't know what?"

"Honestly. I don't know if I trust you yet. I'm sorry. You will get your stones. Just not yet. Apprentice, call a rabbit for your master." Nes'egrinon gave the dead man a little honor by labeling him as such, saying he was still Kerlith's master but everyone knew that was a lie, even the dead man, but it appeased him.

Kerlith rubbed his stone and called. There was not much life here. Not much at all. They were coming closer to the breach and closer to where all was dead and death and decay. Anything living here had been long gobbled up by the stream of dead coming out of the doorway to the underworld. It took quite a while but a small rabbit came and stepped right into the apprentice's hand. By that time Muolithnon's eyes were bulging as he paced back and forth, rubbing his arms and scratching his neck. His skin was the darkest gray. He darted to Kerlith, snatched the bunny from his hand and tore into it. Blood leaked down his cheeks. After a few gulps, color washed back into his face, hands and clothing. He laughed. "That's a rush. I feel almost human." He wiped the red from his lips, smearing it across his cheek. "I know, I know, I'm dead. Okay, I feel much better. Let me just pour the rest of this into my flask. Kind of foul for you to see me do this. You don't have to watch if you don't want to."

Nes'egrinon looked at the two thin boys and said, "Come. We walk. It will be fine."

"Hey, what should I do with the rabbit? Should I

bring it? I should. Maybe I can squeeze more out." The dead man stuffed the dead rabbit in his pocket but his pocket wasn't big enough so the head hung out.

Bel couldn't keep his eyes off the bobbing rabbit head and couldn't keep his mind away from replaying that scene in his mind. He wondered if how he felt was displayed on his face. Doubt and fear. Did it show? Did they know that he was terrified and he thought that they would most surely die soon? He didn't want to be a ghoul and especially not one happily bounding along with a dead rabbit hanging out of his pocket like it was the most normal thing in the world. Dead people should stay dead. That's like, what did they call it at the school? A universal truth? Bel didn't like their situation one bit. But there was nothing he could do about it. He would press on. He would fight. To the death if that's what it took. But he didn't have to like it.

They walked for what felt like a half-day's journey, no one knowing whether it was day or night, and there was less and less trees and more and more rock. The path grew steeper also. They trekked by the light of a single torch and the two boys took turns leading the way. They wanted to conserve oil. No one was to talk, Nes'egrinon told them, and they walked as softly as possible. Sound would travel far in the mountains. Many times the pathway looked to be on the top of the ridge line but they would walk just off of it, down onto one side of the backbone of the hills and mountains so that at least the light would be somewhat blocked from being seen from afar. This made the going much slower because of the uneven terrain and rock. Twisting an ankle out here would mean certain death. Bel longed for the ridge line. At least ghoul-kind couldn't sneak up on them out here in the open, Bel thought.

The dead man grew disoriented more and more quickly so they had to keep stopping and allowing him to drink from his flask. When his flask ran out, he took to wringing the rabbit above his opened mouth. Some more blood came out. It wasn't much but it restored him, at least a little.

Muolithnon spoke, "I know. I know. I can't believe I have to do this. Ah well. Such is life. Hahaha. Or death." His laugh was morbid. No one joined him in it.

Each time they stopped, Kerlith tried to call more rabbits but none came. Then he cast his net wider and called for other creatures. Anything. "Ela, ela, ela." But nothing came. They were surrounded by boulders, rocks and stones; his magic should be strong here, but nothing came.

It felt to Bel like they had been walking for days in what seemed like one long running, continuous dream. A nightmare, really. The silence was so heavy. His ears rang from the lack of sound. It was cold. He knew they would have to sleep soon. They couldn't walk forever. And what then? They would have to take watches. Could he handle a master who decided he was going to drain him, even without his stones? Not likely. And all it took was one bite. A nip even. You couldn't fight the poison. It even took a master. He knew he wouldn't last long if he was bitten. Doubt, fear and now dread seeped from his every pore.

Bel tried to push his mind back to fishing, the ocean and his family but it wouldn't work. Not anymore.

He tried to think about Shireen, but that was worse. He didn't know where she'd been assigned, to what master. He hoped that the ghoul-kind weren't overrunning whatever town or village she was in. He shook his head. He hoped that she yet lived.

The fact that all wizards were prevented from marrying under penalty of excommunication never bothered him. Not until he met her. Not until they fell in love. And her an apprentice too. It seemed like such a stupid rule. But they had to make a choice. Magic or love. Knowledge or emotion. It seemed like a cruel sick joke.

Bel shook his head. Thinking about Shireen wasn't helping. He knew if they didn't do something about the ghoul-kind that they'd all be dead. Even Shireen. He couldn't think about it.

He turned to Kerlith, "So. How're you doing?"

Kerlith looked at him like he was crazy. At least that's what Bel thought but he couldn't be sure, the light was so dim. "Don't worry about it," Kerlith replied.

"When someone says that, there's always something to worry about. That's what my father used to say."

"I don't want to talk about it and I don't care what your father used to say. Just leave me alone."

"Sorry. Just making conversation. It's too quiet out here. Silence is getting on my nerves."

Kerlith huffed then said, "Okay, then let's talk. You want to know how I'm doing? Terrible. My master back there is dead. So now what do I do? I have no master. Yet, he still walks. I can't just leave him; I have to take care of him. But he's a ghoul. What does that make me?"

"Hopefully we can close this breach and send him home."

"We have to try but for me it's all over."

Bel tried to cheer him up, suddenly wishing he wouldn't have started this conversation, "When we close the breach, all the lands will know who did it. You will find a new master then. No problem."

Kerlith seemed suddenly angry. "I know you mean well but at the moment I don't feel like talking about it. Especially not with you. I don't even like you. Sure, we went to school together and I tolerate you sometimes but at the moment I feel like if you fell off this mountain I wouldn't even blink."

"Nice. Real nice. The true Kerlith comes out once again. Can't keep that bottled up too long without letting it out, can you? Hey, I'm sorry your master died. That's a tough break. But don't take it out on me. I had nothing to do with it."

Nes'egrinon hissed, "Keep quiet you two. Don't attract any unwanted attention."

Kerlith ignored the wizard. "I know you had nothing to do with it. But you're here right now." Kerlith flicked his finger and a small stone rose up from the ground and pelted Bel on the face.

Bel wanted to smash him but he knew he couldn't. Kerlith always was kind of irritating, but now, with his master just dying, he had an excuse. "Listen Kerlith, I get the message. You don't want to be bothered. I'll leave you alone. Just quit throwing stones at me."

Kerlith kept walking then shook his hand again. Several rocks popped up and struck Bel.

Bel said, "Why are you being so childish? Stop it."

Kerlith flicked his finger again, tossing a handful more rocks at Bel. One hit him on the bottom lip, cutting it open.

"I've had about enough of you," Bel said as he flashed his staff full of bright white light, pushing all his anger and frustration into it, the anger at watching people who were good and upright reduced to babbling blood-drinking fiends, the rage at watching children run in terror from their dead parents lest they be drained by them, the disappointment at being picked last and somewhat reluctantly and then his first assignment, a suicide mission;

he poured it in, bright white and hot, and the glare shone for miles.

Kerlith smiled broadly as he leapt up the cliff edge, gaining the higher ground, quickly yanking his stone out from behind his shirt, the rock already glowing, tiny flecks of amber-red light swirling around it. He howled, "You want a piece of me? Let's go! I beat you before; I'll do it again!" He swung his arm, stone in hand, down at Bel and a wave rippled out towards him.

Bel didn't know what was coming but he knew that he could reflect it; he made giant arcs above his head with his staff. When the shockwave reached him it was scooped up in the rotation and sent back towards Kerlith. Bel smiled as Kerlith flew into the air. He would have flown off the cliff had not Nes'egrinon stopped him in midair, him pointing his staff at the apprentice, deep concentration twisting the mage's face, his eyes squinted tight.

The wizard bellowed, "Enough!" and somehow the words were not audible but reverberated through Kerlith and Bel's insides, rattling their bones. Nes'egrinon slowly motioned his staff toward the ground and Kerlith, who was hanging still in the air as if suspended by wires, slowly lowered. The mage whispered again, "Can you two stop acting like idiots and just shut up? Like a bunch of babies."

"Babies. Mmmm, yummy," Muolithnon moaned and

they all realized they had to do something about his hunger. Fast.

The old mage stopped and took the dead man's flask. He cut his thumb and drained some of his blood into it as the two boys looked on in disbelief. Nes'egrinon passed the flask to his dead friend and he drank of it eagerly.

The old mage sucked his finger to try to stop the bleeding. "Yuck. I don't know how you like this stuff. But I am getting hungry myself. Hey. Look there." Just over the horizon they could see a halo effect stretching over the far mountain. There was light there.

"Master, what do you think it is?"

"Light. That's for sure. And not from the sun. Torchlight certainly. A lot of them. Just don't know from whom."

Kerlith interjected, "Ghoul-kind? Do you think they would use torches?"

"We don't know much about them do we. Hey. Ghoul. What do you think?"

Muolithnon replied, "You gave me some blood. That's good, but don't call me that."

Nes'egrinon smiled at him.

The dead mage continued, "I don't think so. My eyes actually don't like the light anymore. I feel like I see much better in the dark. It's more comfortable."

"That's good to know. If you have more insights like that, be sure to share. We could use your help you know."

The mage started walking. "We should be able to make that ridge in a morning's journey or so. We'll know more then. We'll go to that area over there. That'll give us a good vantage point, then, if it's safe, we'll head in. Maybe we can get some food. Some shelter and information would be nice too."

Of course he said nothing about what they were all thinking. How can they walk into a town with a ghoul in tow? They couldn't. What were they going to do with him?

They marched on and it didn't feel like they were getting much closer. Bel was growing tired of everything: tired of walking, tired of the darkness and tired of watching a ghoul with a rabbit hanging out of his pocket. He wanted to be anywhere but here walking with this monster towards more monsters who were in all likelihood going to kill them and eat them. Bel drank the last of his water and announced loudly, "Oh well. I'm out of water." He suddenly didn't care if someone heard him.

"Shhh," Kerlith hissed.

"You shhh yourself. I don't want to be here anymore. I hate this place."

Nes'egrinon said, "Kerlith, take the lead. Bel, walk with me."

The lithe boy slowed and passed the torch then walked next to the old hobbling man.

"Fifth Year, you seem a bit on the jittery side. First you promised me that the apprentice over there wouldn't get under your skin and then what? A day later and you two are at each other's throats. Now a little march and you're crying about it. What's going on?"

"I'm not a Fifth Year."

"What?"

"I took six years to graduate," Bel said glumly.

"And you think I didn't know that? Listen son, I've been at this a long time and I don't quite remember what it feels like to be your age but this here, what we're doing, is man stuff. There's no room for whining and acting like a pansy. Now you need to grow a pair real quick because the stuff we're about to face doesn't play kid games. If you blink, you're dead. Understand?"

"I got it." Bel looked at the old man and something changed deep inside of him.

"Now if you got any more sissified concerns then you go ahead and mention them to me and I'll act like I care, maybe for a few seconds anyway, and then we can move on. Now go ahead and get back up there."

Nes'egrinon's harsh words stung but somehow Bel felt better about himself. He was here to train, here to learn, but deep inside he felt like something more was happening; he was giving himself up to the old man. He had always been good at everything he did. Fishing with his father always went well when he was on the boat; they all said he had the gift. When the searchers came, it felt so natural that they would come to his door; it was like he knew it all along; it felt right. Then at Lasaat, all had come easily to him as if it was just a game and he was so good at playing it. There was only the one incident, the one he wanted to forget, and even then he excelled. No one else would have even dared try what he did, not even the masters. Now something deep inside of him was awakening, not by some school boy challenge or an easily accomplished test at the University of Arts and Magic, but by danger and impending doom, by the half-scarred face of an old man long past his years who could cause earthquakes with the slam of his mage-wood staff, by a calm voice full of salty wisdom, by a frail body that could turn into a hawk, a frail body that hobbled slowly behind him and told him to man up.

By the time they reached the far ridge line that jutted over the light source, another half-day's journey had passed, all in silence. Nes'egrinon had to cut his hand two more times and Bel didn't think he should do it again but refused to speak up about it. The old man was looking more and more drained. And they all were tired. They must have been walking for at least a day if not more.

The lights were a sight to behold though. It was a small fortress tucked into the side of a mountain, carved into the rock. A valley sat below it so that all entering must first climb down the mountain and cross the valley to reach the entrance. It was a perfectly designed and perfectly defensible entrance. It was Protolith, the Keep of the stonecutters.

Chapter Ten

Protolith

"Old friend, stay here. We will be back to retrieve you soon," Nes'egrinon said softly as they stared down at the fortress. He could not look at the dead man's face as he spoke.

"Blood," Muolithnon said distantly. Bel realized that Muolithnon did not understand much anymore. More and more his only concern was stopping the gnawing hunger and the longer he went without drinking blood the less human he behaved.

"We're just going to leave him? Out here? On these rocks?" Kerlith asked incredulously.

Bel's shoulders tensed and he gripped his staff harder. He didn't like Kerlith's tone toward his master.

The mage held up his hand at Bel and motioned for

him to calm down. He replied, "Young apprentice, your master asked me to join him on this journey but now it appears that I am leading it. Sometimes I feel like turning around and going back to my forest. This place is so foreign to me; rocks and stones, I cannot understand them, I cannot relate to them. I feel out of place and disjointed. But... here I am. We have gone far and maybe we have a long way to go. What is to become of us? I do not know. Will we be successful? I don't know. But I will tell you this. You are in your lands. You have no tie to me, a forest mage. You can stay here if you like; tend after this man if it is your will. For me and the Fifth Year here, we are going to refresh our supplies, hopefully, down below and continue on. At least for a time. You are welcome to join us but do not feel obligated."

"And my master? Were you planning on taking him with you?"

"I thought it was a good idea when we left the village, but now I cannot say. He needs blood to be of any use to us, but there doesn't seem to be much around, as you well know. I don't think it is a good idea to keep giving him mine."

Bel flinched. He didn't like it either. It was the old idea of association that the creature mages taught him. Never give an animal food out of your hand, especially one that eats meat, because the predator will begin to associate the person with food. His master had already done this and he could see it in Muolithnon's vacant stare that never seemed to leave the dried, caked blood on Nes'egrinon's hand.

Kerlith's face was blank but Bel knew he was troubled.

The gray-haired wizard, having nothing left to say, started down the mountain carefully as the path was dark and full of jagged rocks.

Bel followed, suddenly wanting to eat something and lay in a bed, any bed, even a floor would do right now he was so tired of this endless march.

Kerlith watched them leave then turned to the dead man and said, "I don't know what to do."

"Blood. Some blood. Very hungry."

"Master? Should I stay with you? I don't know what to do."

"Blood. Hungry."

Bel heard them speaking as they climbed down the hill and he was terrified for Kerlith and what he might do. Even though he didn't really like him that much he still thought staying with the dead mage would be a huge mistake.

Kerlith cut his finger and squeezed some blood onto the knife and gave it to the ghoul who eagerly licked it clean.

He quickly changed. "Good. Thank you. Good. I feel like a new... a man. Human. Okay. Listen here. My head's clearing. Give me a moment. Okay, is that? Yes. We're at

Protolith, the Keep of the stonecutters, and is that? Yes, Master Nes'egrinon. He did well. Got us all the way to the Keep, he did."

"Yes, Master."

"Certainly without my help. I think I've been out of it for a while. Last I remember we were still on the forest edge. Okay, listen. I'm dead; remember? I don't want you hanging around here with me. You go after those two and get some food and rest. Here, take that rope and tie me down. When this wears off I'll be out of it and I don't want to get lost where you can't find me. Okay? Hurry up. It's wearing off already."

Kerlith did as the dead man asked but he certainly didn't like it. He felt like he was tying up a dog. It was degrading and he didn't want to do it. But he did. He wrapped the rope around his master's chest and tied it in the back, then around a large boulder and secured it where the mage wouldn't be able to reach either knot in his demented state.

"Okay? I'm going," Kerlith said without a smile.

The mage's skin had already gone gray. "Blood," he said shallowly, looking at Kerlith as if he did not know who he was.

Kerlith turned and began descending the mountain quickly, refusing to allow himself to look back and occasionally wiping the moisture from his eyes, telling himself that he was only sweating. The apprentice caught up to the two just as they reached the base of the mountain and the open field leading up to the fortress entrance.

A voice rang out from an opening above, "Halt! Who approaches?"

Nes'egrinon held out his arms and motioned for them to stop. "I am Nes'egrinon, mage of the western forest, with me are my two assistants. We seek refuge and shelter."

"Hold."

As they waited, Bel studied the fortress. It was lit up with torchlights all around, but the surrounding mountains were quite dark. He found that odd and thought that they would have wanted light surrounding them so that their archers could see their targets if need be. As it was only the castle was lit. Bel turned around and looked back up at the path they just descended and it was pitch black. He knew Muolithnon was there but he couldn't see him. The Protolith sentries wouldn't be able to either. Somehow he was not comforted by that fact as that also meant that they could be surrounded by ghoul-kind tucked into and behind the nooks and crevices of the large boulders and no one would be the wiser.

"Step forward and wait," the sentry hollered out.

The three said nothing and walked into the light and across the open field. After walking by the light of a single torch for so long, the three found the light of thousands of torches to be blinding; they squinted their eyes to slits as they approached. Bel was nervous and didn't want to look up at the archers that had their bead on them. They stopped in front of a large wooden door which had a smaller door inlaid into it. The smaller door opened and the sentry said, "Proceed."

They each stepped through the smaller door into a caged area. The door closed behind them mechanically. On the other side of the cage was a group of soldiers looking them over. One said, "What business do you have here, wood-mage?"

Kerlith stepped forward, "Alexius, it is I, Kerlith, apprentice to Master Muolithnon, the wizard of these lands. You remember me, don't you?"

"Aye. Kerlith, it is good to see you here. We have been without anyone of decent magical ability for a time. A lot has happened since you and your master left these parts some weeks ago. We are at our wits end. So you brought a forest-mage with you, ay? What has become of your master?"

Kerlith looked at the floor. "He does not live."

"Aye. I suspected as much when I didn't see him at your side. It's a hard time for all of us and I'm sorry to hear this. Forest mage, my apologies for keeping you in this cage but please, let me call the king and I'll be right back with his word of release." The head guard quickly trotted away. The other guards stood silent as it was not in the stone people's nature to take to much talking but they did seem glad to see that people of magic were about.

Alexius returned and unlocked the cage, saying, "Sorry for the delay. No one knows what is day or night anymore. The king was in his bed. I'll take you to clean yourselves and let you make yourselves presentable and then to see the king. He would like word of your journey and the things you have seen." Bel thought that it might be a long time before he would be able to sleep and the idea drained him.

The guard led the three down several unlit, damp and slimy hallways. The Keep felt like a dungeon which was unpleasant for Bel who had only known the wide openness of the ocean and the embrace of the trees in the forest. He felt as if the large, cut stones forming the walls and ceiling were bearing down on him. When they reached the door to a room, Bel unconsciously placed his hand on the wood and caressed it. Nes'egrinon looked at him and said, "I know. I feel it to. It will pass."

Kerlith, not understanding, said, "Feel what?" but no one answered him and they all went into the room and began disrobing, bathing and cleaning themselves. The room was small but nicely appointed and in the corner was a mirror, which struck them all as odd. Bel thought the room must only be for visiting royalty. He looked at himself in it and saw a grim, dirty, gaunt face staring back. He knew who it was but somehow could not believe that in such a short time he could degrade so quickly. After they washed themselves and knocked the majority of the dust and grime off their clothing they put their clothes back on and opened the door.

Alexius said, "Follow me."

The long hallway led to a chamber with two more guards and a door. Passing through the door, they entered a large open room with a cathedral ceiling made of intricate crystal glasswork. Kerlith seemed to glow in there. At the end of the room was the king's chair but he did not sit in it; he stood nearby looking out of an open window into the darkness. Nes'egrinon stopped about three paces away and waited.

The king did not turn from his dark view but said, "My name is Luthgar. Welcome, mage of the forest. Our peoples of recent times have been on peaceful terms and with what is now happening now I can only assume that this situation is what has drawn you from your forest?"

"Yes, good king. My name is Nes'egrinon and you speak correctly. My people have been afflicted by this darkness just as yours have here and we intend to continue on to its source. We will try to stop it. We request whatever aid you can provide us."

"Yes, yes. Alexius, see to it." The king turned and looked at them. "Kerlith I know and have met. Yes, you look quite haggard young apprentice. I am sorry to hear that our mage is not with the living. Is it so?"

Kerlith said, "Aye, it is so."

The king spoke, "It is a sad day when we lose one such as him. When this is over we will mourn him properly. I suppose that he is about? Like the others?"

Kerlith started but Nes'egrinon spoke first, "In this eternal darkness the dead do not stay dead. It is beyond understanding. He is dead, yet he walks about. He is a ghoul, like the others. Have you had many attacks of ghoul-kind here in this grand fortress?"

"Aye. More than you know. On a typical day our gates are open and welcoming. People come and go from the quarries and village traders enter, as they like. On the first day of the darkness... Day, huh, I still use that term but somehow it has become foreign to me. No matter. On the first day, the morning light was bright and lively as it always is, then, suddenly, it was as if someone was blotting out the noonday sun and a sort of twilight came over the land. Everyone thought it to be storm-sign so the people pulled in the carts and trailers to be covered. In retrospect we should have known something was awry because there were no clouds. No rain came. No harsh winds. The sun was just... gone. The next day, the stars left us and that is when the ghoul-kind flooded into the valley."

Kerlith said, "Sounds like there were lots of them."

"A lot? Thousands. They came in, some so oddly dressed that our sentries did not know what to make of it and did not sound an alarm or close the gates. They carried no weapons; they did not seem threatening. Most of them just meandered around babbling about being hungry. We tried to feed them thinking that they were the peoples of some yet undiscovered land that must have suffered some cataclysmic hardship for such a large number of them to show up all at once like that. Their skin was gray, sure, so we thought that they were from afar. We had no idea they were ghoul-kind."

"I see," Nes'egrinon replied.

"They wouldn't eat anything we put before them: grain meal, fruits or vegetables. Even water they would not drink! Then, after these people, many who were already inside our gates, began to ask for blood my people became quite nervous. We couldn't understand what manner of people these were who constantly complained of being hungry, refused to eat then asked to only drink blood. No. It was insanity upon insanity. Then one of them bit one of the maids."

"Sounds like a bad situation, King Luthgar," Nes'egrinon said.

"Aye. Don't get me wrong. Most of the ghoul-kind don't attack. They just mill around in a kind of stupor, complain of their hunger and ask for blood. Pretty harmless actually. But some few of them—a small group, really—were quite aggressive and bit some of my people."

"Yes, yes. We have had some dealings with some such as these as well. How did you handle it?" Nes'egrinon replied.

"The guards pushed them out with sword and spear, out into the outer court yard and then out into the approach valley. Many continued to wander off into the mountains. Some did not want to leave though and then a handful of them attacked my men. They had no recourse but to defend themselves. They cut them. They hit them with their swords. Then the oddest thing happened. One of the ghoul's arms was cut off but no blood came out. The dead man bent down, picked up the arm and began to swing it like a sort of a club. At that sight some of my men ran to the court and secured the inner gate. It was then that we knew they were ghoul-kind."

"That's a bad way to find out such a truth. Did you lose many to their poison?" the wizard said.

The king continued, "Aye. Pretty much all the people in the outer ring. And the maid who was first bitten. I watched her go. But it wasn't long. When she rose up after she died it gave us quite a start. But she was a soft soul. She asked to go out and we let her down the wall."

"And the rest?" the old mage asked.

"They tried to gain access but it didn't take long for us to realize that fire was our best weapon against them. Hot oil and fire. We waited many days before the majority moved on. The small bands of stragglers were harder to deal with."

"Oh? Really?" Nes'egrinon said as he furrowed his brow.

"Aye. The foreigners, the long dead, the people not of this land moved on quickly. The ones who stayed behind were the recently dead from the Keep, my people, the people who we had so recently saw, spoke and ate with; children, fathers, mothers, sisters and brothers. It was very difficult."

"How did you get them to leave?" Kerlith asked.

"We tried all manner of things but in the end, I spoke to them. I asked them to leave. I told them who they were. Somehow, they could not stand to hear it, to hear the truth."

The wizard said, "I see. And then you were able to secure the outer courts and the gates. And no attacks since?"

The king replied somberly, "Not even any sightings of ghoul-kind in some few days. But still this night does not leave us. We were not sure what you were when you approached."

"I see," Nes'egrinon said but his mind seemed suddenly elsewhere as if he was pondering a riddle.

The king asked, "And you, my forest mage, you have traveled far. Tell me of what you have seen in your journey. Does this darkness spread over all the lands?"

Nes'egrinon told the king of how the darkness appeared in the forest, the visit of Muolithnon and their travels and many battles with the ghoul-kind. He told them that he intended to find its source and either close the breach himself or call more wizards to his aid. He tried to sound as confident as possible as if the situation was completely under control. He continued, "So it appears that we are heading in the right direction as master Muolithnon reported experiencing the darkness and the ghoul-kind long before it reached my forest. By the way, have any other wizards passed through here before us?"

The king answered quickly, "No, you are the first." He then returned to his window and said, "My father before me ruled this land and his father before him. Twelve generations back we go, keeping this land, watching over it and caring for this people. All the while we have always taken council of the magical folk, as that is our way. Seers, mage folk like yourselves, and others who might give us a little wisdom or insight into the comings and goings of the lands and peoples around us and perhaps even into the depths of what is to come. But this. No. Not one of them warned us of this. Here, at Protolith, we are losing confidence in the ways of magic. Do you really think you will be able to stop this?"

Bel did not know the mannerisms of the old man well but he knew that something was troubling him. Perhaps his master thought the king was hiding something. Bel felt it too. He was well trained in the magic of discerning speech. It is much more than reading body language or facial expressions but being able to see the metaphysical source of a person's words. He closed his eyes and began to focus himself on the king, blocking out everything else around him.

"King Luthgar, I thank you for your honesty so I will be honest in return. I don't know. All I can do is go and see. Try to discover the source of this phenomenon. Maybe we can do nothing. Maybe this is the beginning of the end of the world. I do not know what will come but all I can do is try."

The room was silent for a long time so Nes'egrinon said, "Very well. If you have no further questions, it has been quite a long journey. I ask your leave, your majesty."

"Yes, yes. Go. Rest. Alexius, please see that our guests are well fed and their room has all they require."

The group followed Alexius back out through the narrow corridors. As they walked Bel desperately wished to ask his master about the words the king said and what he felt about them. He wanted to know what his master thought and if he also felt that the king was hiding something and if so, what and why. But he knew the walls had ears here. All castles did. There would be no way they could have an open conversation in these halls or rooms. He would have to wait until they left and maybe then it would be too late. He was also tired, extremely tired, and really wanted to be in bed.

They entered a small dining hall and ate some bread with soup and a few pieces of fruit. Kerlith ate the fruit eagerly and said that unlike the Greenlands it was a delicacy here. They ate mostly in silence. After their quick meal, they were led back to the room and then fell asleep quickly. Bel did not sleep well as the one-armed boy invaded his dreams.

The next day Bel was awakened by Kerlith who always made too much noise. His master was already up also and cleaning himself. Bel rose and while he packed his sack asked, "Master, do we continue on today?"

"I want to get this over with as soon as possible. Yes, we go today. Kerlith, you have a short time to decide if you will be accompanying us."

The apprentice replied, "I won't need any more time. I'm coming with you."

"Fine. Just make sure you're coming for the right reason. This isn't going to be about vengeance, you know. I just want to get this breach closed."

"Revenge? Sure I want revenge but don't worry, my feelings won't get in the way," Kerlith replied.

Nes'egrinon added, "Don't get me wrong. Vengeance is fine. I've been known to lay out a little retribution in my day too, but right now I don't want anyone getting blinded by it. We are only a few and we need to keep focused."

Kerlith continued, "Nothing I can do will bring him back. But what I can do is help send him home. Help him to stop being a ghoul. If I go with you I can tend to him also. You are still going to bring him, right?"

"I suppose. After we eat, you can check the kitchen and see if they have any blood drippings we can flask for him."

"Yes, Master Nes'egrinon."

Bel felt sorry for Kerlith and even though he didn't like him, he thought it would be good to have him on the journey, especially now that they were in the stone lands. A rap at the door interrupted Bel's thoughts. He opened it to see a distraught Alexius.

"Come. Please. We are under attack by the ghoul-kind. Please. The king has requested your assistance."

Chapter Eleven

Ghoul Attack

The three followed Alexius out quickly, turning this way and that through the catacomb-like tunnels eventually pouring out onto an upper landing overlooking the outer courtyard of the Keep. There were ghoul-kind everywhere down below, leaping from the shadows, grabbing maids and merchants and pulling them into corners and small structures, tackling warriors long enough to bite them and carefully avoiding the edge of the wall where the oil and fire might be poured. Bel and Kerlith peered over the edge as the archers fired their crossbows.

Nes'egrinon said, "How? How did they get in?"

Alexius replied, "I suspect the people of Protolith, the recently dead, knew some way in. Tunnels? Pipes? Many of them were military but others, craftsmen: metal workers, people who fix things, others who cleaned the aqueducts that brought the water, people who spent a lot of time in the underbelly of this fortress. All I can think is that they knew its secrets; they knew how to get in. This had to be planned out."

"I see. And where is King Luthgar?"

"There," Alexius said, pointing at a landing overhead. "He oversees the battle there."

"Take me to him. Kerlith, Fifth Year, you two stay here. Help as you can but do not go down the wall."

The two nodded. Kerlith pulled out his stone quickly as Alexius and Nes'egrinon walked away. Alexius led the mage up a steep staircase and passed four guards at the top. King Luthgar met them.

"Archmage, we need your help," the king said.

"Yes, I know. Look below, my two companions are already working." Nes'egrinon pointed at Bel and Kerlith who were together speaking into the souls of the dead, telling them to sleep, to rest, calming their spirits, reminding them that they are not of the living and should not be here. They sent it out in wave after wave, bombarding the ghoul-kind with this simple message. Confusion stole over many of the ghouls as they stopped and looked about, unsure, bewildered, then stared down at themselves and their blood-soaked arms and legs. Some began to leave, their shoulders slumped down low, longing to return to the earth and their rest. But many others stayed.

"Yes, yes. Good. And will you not join them?" the king asked.

"Might I have a word alone?"

Luthgar looked at the mage warily then said, "Alexius, give us a moment."

The chief of guards put his hand on the hilt of his sword and snapped his heels then retreated to the far guard station.

Nes'egrinon whispered, "I will help you and I appreciate you helping us on our journey but I must ask you this..." The old mage paused, suddenly unsure of how to phrase his next sentence. He had always been one to blurt out exactly what he was feeling but that, right now, would certainly be an insult. And to a king no less. He knew he needed his help and he knew he was completely out of his rights to ask for it; he was a woodland mage in the land of the stonecutters. It had been a long time since their people were at war but both the king and the mage were old enough to remember it. Nes'egrinon wanted to be subtle and show tact but he had no idea how. The old mage threw up his hands and spoke, "It's like this. I know you were lying to me. I just don't get it. Did you think I wouldn't know? I am one of the oldest living archmages in all the lands. Why'd you lie to me? That pretty foolish."

"What? How dare you speak to me so!"

Alexius started towards them.

The old mage said, "Fine. I'm leaving. Deal with your dead as you see fit."

"Wait. Wait. Alexius, we are fine. Come Master Archmage, walk with me. Here, over here, we can speak more privately here."

He led the mage to a more secluded corner of the overlook so that his guards could not overhear their conversation. The king stopped and stared at the mage and he stared back. The gray-haired wizard's scarred face looked haggard in the torchlight and the king could not hold his eyes upon him. It was something about his eyes, the deep-set orbs that stared back at him, into him and through him, looking down into his very soul; he could not look into them for long; it was as if in the depths of his eyes he saw a reflection of himself, distorted, somehow a reflection that displayed his true nature, the man inside, and he did not like the image.

The King looked at his feet and said, "Yes, I lied. There was a group of mages that passed through here before you. Master Rylithnon and a few others, all from the wizard school in the west. Lasaat, I believe it is called? They passed through here a few weeks ago."

"And?"

"And I lied about that. I am sorry. But my people, you can help rid us of these ghouls?"

"I could help. But you're still not telling me

everything. Why?"

The king turned to look down at the battle. It was not going well. He replied, "A cheery lot, them. They were quite excited to be going in. Rylithnon promised me some things, magical items. And to teach me to wield them."

"Then he lied to you. Only those who are called can wield."

"Perhaps, but I had to take the chance. Never has a magician king sat on this throne. You know it is an uneasy alliance, kings and wizards. You know it. It is not rare for mage-kind to overthrow kings and kingdoms—"

The old mage cut his words in the air, "Yes, and perhaps they are justified. Not all kings have the lives of their people in mind." Nes'egrinon recalled a kingdom or two that he helped overthrow and the memory brought bile into his mouth. He did not know if Luthgar knew his history though.

"Aye. But who is the judge? A mage? There is much more to politics than right and wrong and the concern of the people. I have had to make many a tough choice in my rule and not everyone thinks I did right but my conscience is free."

The archmage spoke slowly, as if the wheels in his mind were turning, figuring something out that he could not quite piece together. "I know that now. But tell me then, what excited them? And what did you give them for these promises?"

"Their excitement? I don't know. I didn't ask. Their promises were enough for me and they didn't ask for much. Some supplies, much like you have asked. I would have given it to them readily even without their promises. I have always been a friend to the mage-kind."

"So you say. Very well then. I'll ask one last thing. I'll help you to clear your streets of these ghoul-kind. Have your men ready to secure the tunnels or pipes or aqueducts or whatever they used to sneak into the Keep. Then, when we leave, you will give us some horses and some men, perhaps four or five, a few warriors, to aid us on our journey."

"I'll ask for volunteers. I think it won't be a problem."

"And one other thing. I want Alexius to accompany us."

"What? My chief of guards? No, no, no. He is vital to —"

"I understand he is vital to the Keep but if we don't end this darkness you'll not have a Keep to rule. I need someone I can trust to lead the men. A warrior and a leader. I need someone that your men will follow. I am certain they will not follow me. No soldier has ever trusted a wizard."

"A wizard of the forest wants to take away the stonecutters' chief of guard, eh?"

"Listen to me! This is not a plot on your kingdom! You stone people are all alike. Quick like rock. Dumb like rock. I'm trying to help you here! Think!"

Luthgar hissed, "I do not like your tone! If we stood here on another day, in the brightness of daylight, I would have your head. But since it appears I have no choice you will have what you request. Now go. Do your job, mage."

The archmage walked away, past Alexius and the four guards and down the steps. Alexius followed. Upon reaching the lower level Nes'egrinon peered over the wall next to Bel and Kerlith. "How goes it?" He quizzed.

Bel quickly replied, "We have been telling them to rest. Using the old language. It is working but only on a limited scale. Some of the stragglers and the ones who did not seem to be so committed have left, down through that far grating there. Can you see it? Also the newly dead, the ones just killed today, they left also. They were disoriented and were easy to scatter."

"I see. Alexius, would it be possible for us to put a force on this end of the circle and push the ghoul-kind back toward that grating?"

"There is an entrance there on that side, yes. But if we open it and the ghouls get in, we could lose the inner court. We would have to be quick. We would have to open it, get the men out and then close the door behind. There would be no retreat if the forces fell."

"I will lead the charge then."

"Master?" Bel said shallowly, but he knew not what question to ask, only that a dread was choking him and he didn't know how to stop it. He didn't want to lose his master too; he did not want to be in Kerlith's position, an apprentice with no master.

"You two stay here. Keep doing what you're doing. Alexius, come gather your men." Nes'egrinon began to walk away then stopped and turned back. "By the way Kerlith, I've been watching you. You understand that when you give into rage that you're inviting darkness into your heart, don't you? Maybe this is too obvious to say but darkness cannot defeat darkness." Nes'egrinon spun on his heel without another word and followed Alexius down the far staircase and Bel watched their backs disappear.

"Hey stupid," Kerlith said with irritation in his voice. "Snap out of it. We need to keep that area clear for when they open the door."

Bel bristled at Kerlith's name calling but ignored it and began reciting the words in the language of the ancients, again calling for the dead to rest and return to their graves in the earth, pointing his staff down at them, trying to concentrate the direction and placement of the magic as he rotated his staff in the air. But Bel had quite enough of Kerlith's big mouth and his constant insults so he decided that even though they were working together at the moment he was going to let him know what he thought about him, "Listen Kerlith, we're working together, okay? That's good but I don't appreciate your childish name calling."

Kerlith continued to focus his magic down onto the ghoul-kind without responding. Below, the far door opened and about twenty men rushed out with swords and torches. Nes'egrinon was in front and Alexius at the rear. The door slammed behind them and the sound echoed in Bel's ears. Bel spoke again as he continued to send out his magic, "So if we are going to work together it is generally a bad idea to keep trying to poke your partner in the eye with your verbal stick."

Kerlith snickered as he continued to push the magic down at the ghoul-kind. "Agreed, unfortunately this job is going to take both of us. I got my side. Just make sure your weak magic takes care of yours."

"What? That's exactly what I'm talking about. You insignificant louse! You water flea! Weak? You're the whelp. Even though we are in the land of stone I could still take you out!"

"With what? A wiggle? Are you going to wiggle and fart on me? Ooh, now that's got me scared."

"I'll be fine. Believe me. You got out of Lasaat a year before me and you have a year more training than I do so maybe you might give me a little work out. I may have to exercise more than my little finger to smack you down."

Kerlith stopped laughing and focused on the ghoul-kind below. His magic began to build and the longer and harder he pushed the more his anger boiled over. He was feeding it and feeding off of it. Rage feeding rage and the magic he was pouring out on the ghoul-kind below increased exponentially in ferocity. He growled, "When this is all over, I'm coming at you."

"You'll die trying," Bel said calmly. He didn't mind the idea of putting Kerlith in his place once and for all after all he had suffered because of him. He wasn't going to look for it but if Kerlith came at him then he would fight him again when this was all over. For now he would play nice as his master had requested.

Nes'egrinon filled the end of his staff with a purple glowing haze and Bel and Kerlith knew it was the love magic that the ghouls ran from at Sha'ane Village. He was concentrating it in the end of his staff and using the staff as a club. Swinging the staff anywhere near a ghoul would send it screaming and wailing as it ran away to the far end of the outer court. The soldiers followed closely behind using torches, swords and shields on the ghoul-kind that occasionally leapt from the shadows or rooftops.

A soldier who was nearly bitten yelled, "Master archmage, our swords have little effect. Should we abandon them for the torches?"

The mage quickly looked back then returned his focus at the approaching dead. He swung his staff a few more times at the ghouls then replied, "Cut their heads off. They can't attack if they can't see."

The soldiers swung their swords in earnest, taking more and more ground and soon a small pile of heads sat in the center of the ring. They had gained control over half of the outer court.

The eyes on the piled-up heads looked about and some of them spoke, "Hey that's not right. You cut off my head!"

Another said, "All we wanted was a little blood!"

One other said, "Now where'd my body go? Oh, over there. There you are. Now get over here and pick me up."

Alexius howled, "Men. Get those heads and throw them down that far drain. Carefully, carefully. They still bite you know."

The heads continued to speak while the men threw them down the large opening in the floor. "Hey! That's not nice!"

The head of an elderly woman said, "Sonny, I remember when you were in diapers. Wore them until you were in school, you did. And this is how you treat me now?"

Another howled, "Don't forget my body! Send it down too. I'm gonna need that!"

The men pitched all of the heads down the large storm drain. Then they pushed the headless bodies down the pipe, poking and prodding them with their swords to get them to walk where they wanted them to, guiding them to the opening.

It took about a quarter day but they were able to clear the outer court of all the ghoul-kind and place large stones over all of the open drains and open pipes that they found. The king ordered the outer court secured and they opened up the passages but many would not yet venture there. Others did, if only to retrieve the memorabilia and keepsakes of their friends and kin who had now joined the ghoul-kind. There was no celebration in their victory.

Chapter Twelve

Alexius And His Band

Soon after the outer court was cleared, King Luthgar announced, "All, gather round. Please. Please, gather round. Hear what your king would say to you."

Once the people gathered and quieted, he began. "Another battle we have won and I join you in mourning our lost once again. Now we look to a day when this eternal night would end, a day when the ghoul-kind would leave us, a day when the dead would stay dead. We look to the return of day and its life-giving light. These strangers to our lands, these wizards who have helped us, desire to leave us and seek the source of the ghoul-kind and this dreadful eternal darkness. My heart and prayers go with them that they might find the source of this abomination and rid us of it once and for all."

A resounding "Aye" rang out from the stonecutters of the Keep.

"Now my people, I ask your help once again. This is hard. Once again, on this day, we have lost mothers, fathers, sisters and brothers. We cannot let this be for naught, my friends. I am asking you all to consider aiding them on their quest. A handful of men, that is all they require. But consider it carefully for it may very well be a dangerous journey."

None raised their hands or stepped forward so after a time the king called Alexius to him and said privately, "Old friend, perhaps you might lead a group of your fellows?"

Alexius looked into the king's eyes and saw that he wanted him to decline the offer. It was another one of the king's political shows; he knew it, but he also knew the importance of the mission and that none of the soldiers would volunteer without him.

Alexius turned from the king, stepped forward and announced to the people, "I, Alexius, will go. I will join myself with the mage-kind. I will follow them into the depths of the abyss and the mouth of the underworld. I will go with them. I will help them to end this eternal darkness before both it and the ghoul-kind consume us all.

I, Alexius, will go. Perhaps I will not return but let it be know now and on this day that a guard of Protolith, a simple man of the stonecutters, walked out into the darkness, faced the ghoul-kind and the dead of the underworld and attempted to do what no other man has ever done. Let it be known and carved in the stone of our histories that his name was Alexius."

The group of guards howled, "Aye!"

A soldier stepped forward saying, "I will follow you!" Then another. Then another likewise. In the end nine stepped forward. Alexius addressed them, "My people, look upon these men of courage and valor who have stepped forward on such a mission as this. I wish I could take them all but I would let El decide."

The chief of guards pulled out straws, cutting three shorter and tucking them deep into his palm. The nine men drew lots. Three men drew shorter sticks than the rest.

The soldiers gathered horses and some supplies and Alexius led Nes'egrinon and the boys back to their room to retrieve their belongings then out to the outer gate where the men were waiting with the horses.

The mage whispered to Kerlith, "Did you stop in the kitchen as I asked?"

"Yes, Master Archmage. All is as you requested," Kerlith replied while tapping one of his flasks hanging from his shoulder.

Nes'egrinon announced, "Very well then. Men, this is your last chance to turn back. Where we are going is fraught with danger; I cannot guarantee your safety and neither can Alexius. All I can say is that if someone does not go to find the source of this eternal night and close the gateway to the underworld then this will never end and we will all die."

He paused and looked at each of them who each replied, "Aye," in turn. They were all committed; they all knew the risks. Then Nes'egrinon looked at Kerlith. "And you, young apprentice. I will tell you once more, you can stay here and there would be no dishonor. The people of the Keep could use a magician right now. You would be of much help to them."

"I thank you for your consideration Master Archmage, but I will continue on." Bel saw the look on Kerlith's face, a sort of contorted discomfort as if he was barely holding back a sense of rage just under the surface of his skin, it wanting to bubble up and boil over. He saw it earlier too, when they both were on the landing working on the ghoul-kind below, anger mixed in with a smile, a rage married to joy; it was the sweet taste of revenge which can never satiate the pain of loss. He was punishing the ghoul-kind for the death of his master. Although Bel never experienced anything like what Kerlith was going through, he thought he could almost understand it. He just hoped that Kerlith's rage didn't affect the mission. His master had said that darkness could not defeat darkness. Bel didn't really understand that since all magic was composed of life and light but still he wondered if something black in Kerlith's heart could bite them in the end. Maybe that is why my master keeps offering Kerlith a chance to quit.

Nes'egrinon mounted his horse and the two boys followed suit. The gates opened and they rode out into the large open space in front of the fortress. The old mage said, "You all go that way. I must retrieve something in the mountains. I'll join you all momentarily. Kerlith, come with me. Fifth Year, be on guard. Have your staff ready."

Before anyone could say another word, the two were off. Alexius said, "Very well then. We ride. I'll take the lead. Be ready for the way is dark." Without Nes'egrinon with them, Bel suddenly felt naked. Perhaps the others did too. The soldiers followed Alexius but having one of the most storied archmages in their group had to have given many of them some additional confidence to join this mission. Now they were five feet out of Protolith and he had already left them.

The horses trotted along the dark winding road around the back side of the mountain that the Keep was carved into. It wasn't long before they could no longer see it, although the vertical horizon formed from thousands of lit torches shining past the side of the mountain reminded them of where it was. They continued on, mostly in silence, each of the soldiers taking turns leading for a period of time. Bel stayed in the middle of the pack, eyes aware, darting to any hint of motion behind boulders and large rocks that they passed. But nothing moved here, at least not when he stared; there were no trees, no animals and no life here, only rock and dirt and stone. Bel could not understand how a wizard could live in these lands and feel whole.

"Ho! Here they come," one of the soldiers near the rear of the band announced.

They all stopped and turned their horses to look back at two riders on horseback, no, it was three riders on two horses.

Another soldier said, "What's this? They've brought along someone."

Alexius said, "Let's keep moving. They'll catch up soon."

Sometime later, Nes'egrinon and Kerlith caught them. Seated behind Kerlith was Muolithnon, the hood of his cloak pulled up over his head, him slouched down as if he was sleeping.

The two quickly folded into the group coming up alongside of Bel and just behind the lead soldier. The others and Alexius were all in the rear and some began to mumble to each other.

Nes'egrinon said, "Fifth Year, any problems?"

"I haven't even seen anything move. Nothing. All is dead here. Inanimate. Nothing lives." His voice sounded hollow, as if the idea drained him.

"I know. It grabs my heart close. Something is in the air here. The closer we come, the stronger I feel it. We must keep strong. Do not let it control you."

Alexius trotted up and said to his man, "I'll lead. Go back with the others." After the lead soldier left to the back, Alexius looked at the mage then sped up and put a little distance between them.

Nes'egrinon followed suit and came up next to him. "What's wrong? Men grumbling?"

"You know it. They want to know who you have there. Please don't tell me it's a ghoul."

The wizard stayed quiet.

Alexius waited for a response and not receiving one he asked, "You're not going to answer me?"

"You told me not to tell you he was a ghoul."

"So he's a ghoul then?"

"You told me not to tell you. Make up your mind. Do you want to know or don't you?"

"I do."

Nes'egrinon said plainly, "Okay then. He's a ghoul. That's all your men need to know."

"Are you serious? This is going to put a real strain on my ability to lead these men, you know. I mean it's bad enough I asked them to travel with magicians. You know how nervous soldiers can be when they are around mage-kind. Now a ghoul too? What's next, giants and orcs?"

"Alexius, I don't know what to tell you. If your soldiers are scared then we don't need them."

The men behind started grumbling louder and Alexius and Nes'egrinon realized that they could still hear their conversation, at least some of it anyway.

The wizard continued, "Listen. Me and mine will stay to one side, you and yours to the other. We can camp separately too. Okay?"

Alexius said, "I don't like this but it will have to do."

As the chief of guards moved to the back to calm his men, the archmage muttered, "The story of my life. I'm surrounded by pansies. It's like they keep multiplying. Not a real man among the lot of them."

Muolithnon groaned, "Blood."

The old wizard quickly said, "Kerlith! Keep him quiet! Pass him the flask, just don't let him drink too much at once."

The apprentice allowed his dead master a gulp every couple thousand paces or so and he began to get a feel for the rhythm of the dead man's thirst. Each time the dead man drank Nes'egrinon would quickly ask him what he felt, if they were getting closer, if he could feel the presence of the breach, if he could sense ghoul-kind about, anything to get a feeling how their progress was going.

"Aaaarrgh!" screamed a ghoul as he leapt out from behind a large boulder. Bel's staff brightened as he spoke in the old tongue, "Apokrothos!" flinging the ghoul far into the air, him screaming all the way, then landing in a thud in the distance.

"Good job, Fifth Year," his master said without looking at him.

The soldiers grumbled less thereafter.

They continued on for a half-day's journey, repelling an occasional attacking ghoul, then stopped to eat some rationed morsels and let the horses drink water. After a short stay, they remounted and rode on for a time until Alexius called for their night's rest, saying only that the horses needed to recuperate, but truthfully they all did.

The men piled large stones into an arc to give a meager break from the cold wind and they huddled behind them and tried to sleep some. Nes'egrinon, the two boys and the dead man set up camp about twenty-five feet away, close enough that the soldiers could keep their eyes on them but not so close that they would not have time to draw their swords, not that swords could stop a mage. The old wizard thought that it would give them a little peace, even if it were a false comfort.

Kerlith built their wall by hand, having calculated the amount of energy he would expend using magic versus the amount used in manual labor, knowing that he could do it in a few moments using magic but not wanting to expend so much life-force in a place where it could not be easily replenished.

After they ate, Alexius joined the mages for some

words. "My men, they are not bad. They are tough, fearless men. Trust me, I have fought many a battle at their sides."

Nes'egrinon and the others looked up at him not knowing how to respond.

Alexius continued, "It's just that there have been too many stories about mage-kind. You know, talking to dragons, other stories of some aiding the orcs, overthrowing the kingdoms of men, you know the ones. These men have all been told stories by their nurse maids from their youth and in some such stories the mage-kind are the monster in the closet or under the bed. They are fearless men. True. But it is hard for them to trust what they do not understand."

The mage looked down wearily. "Do not let it trouble you. We are fine over here." He then looked up, smiled and said, "I don't care if they are pansies, I am sure they will do their duty when the time has come."

Alexius said, "Right," clearly not liking the fact that his men might hear the old man's insults, then walked back to his group and grabbed a spot against the short stonewall, curling his body into a tight ball and pulling his cloak tight.

They fell asleep quickly but the wind, the cold and Muolithnon's occasional cries for blood woke them often. No one slept well that night.

Sometime later Alexius shook everyone awake and

they all mounted their horses. The path quickly became more treacherous for the horses, especially in the dark as they could not always see exactly where they were placing their feet. After another half-day's journey the path became much steeper and Nes'egrinon called back, "Alexius, does any in your band know this path? Does it continue to get worse?"

"Aye," he replied. "We all know it. Soon we must leave the horses. They'll not be able to take us into these mountains."

It was not much longer when he called for them to dismount and they argued about tying the horses to a boulder.

One soldier said, "If we tie them, then they will be here for us when we return."

"When?" another said. "You can't leave them here alone for days with no water. And what of the ghoul-kind?"

In the end they decided to let the horses loose. The horses should be able to find their way back to Protolith. Hopefully they would make it without being attacked by ghoul-kind.

They continued walking on foot and the going was much slower as the path, if you could call it that, was full of jagged, ankle-gashing rocks. It would be hard enough to traverse in daylight but in the constant black, it was nearly impossible. Kerlith occasionally called a dim light into the surrounding stones when the way was especially treacherous but tried to not do it too much as it drained energy from all of them and he was nervous about weakening them before they even knew what they were up against.

Kerlith tied Muolithnon's hand to his shoulder but as he had less and less blood to give him, the dead man stumbled often and the going was slow. His responses to Nes'egrinon's questions were becoming less helpful too; they just didn't have enough blood to give him in order to flush the fog from his dead brain. The group found themselves having to stop more and more often to allow them to catch up. Then the flask of blood ran out. As the band was waiting for Kerlith and his master to reach them, Alexius spoke openly to the archmage, "Nes'egrinon, do you feel it wise to continue so? Do you see this ghoul aiding us that much that it is worth risking this mission?"

"I have thought on this for some time and you are right to question. Let me speak to him."

The men's eyes stared hard at the mage and gave space when Kerlith and Muolithnon arrived.

Nes'egrinon said loudly, "Kerlith, has the flask run dry?"

"Yes, Master Archmage. Perhaps only a few drops left."

The dead man mumbled incoherently, "Blood. Blood. Please. Give blood."

"Give it to him."

Kerlith untied his master's hand and passed him the flask. The dead man slurped and sucked on it until not a drop remained. The soldiers looked away in disgust.

Nes'egrinon placed his hand on the dead man's shoulder and said, "My old friend, how goes it?"

"I… I don't know. Need more blood. My mind is not yet clear."

"Can you tell us? Are we close? Can you feel the pull?"

"Ay… Aye. Oooh, my head. We are close. Can I have a little more blood?"

The archmage pressed, "Please tell me. What do you see? Do you know what is ahead? What do you feel?"

"I feel… magic. There is magic here. I… I… Can I have… blood? Blood. Need blood." The dead man's mind was gone again.

Nes'egrinon looked at Kerlith. "Apprentice, we must leave him. We have no more blood and we cannot give him ours. You must let him go."

"But master? I cannot. I am sworn to him."

"Listen! He's dead! Got it! You have to leave him. If we are successful then he will return to the earth. If we take him then I see our chances are much less. Think, son. We fail and he stays like this. We must leave him."

Kerlith's eyes started to tear. "But Master Archmage, he has been helping us. He has been showing us the way."

"What you say is true but that is not the reason you say it. We are close enough now, anyway. I know you feel the pull. Certainly the Fifth Year can feel it too."

Bel didn't like being dragged into this painful moment but he nodded anyway.

The wizard continued, "You feel it; he feels it; I feel it. What do we need Muolithnon for now? He's dead. Let him go. In his condition he cannot help us and he is slowing us down."

Everyone looked at the indecision on the young apprentice's face. If he decided to stay with the dead man then they would not stop him but they all knew it would only lead to his death.

Finally Kerlith turned to the dead man and spoke, "Master? I must leave you now. I must leave you to wander."

"Blood. Need blood," he replied vacantly.

"Master, please. I would ask of your stones. Your ring, it is on my finger. I would like to keep it; perhaps it will help me… help us to close the breach, to help send you home."

"Need… blood."

Kerlith began to slide the ring from his finger then the archmage placed his hand on his shoulder and said, "Keep it. We need everything we can." The mage spun the boy around and cupped him into his shoulder, saying, "Let's go now. Don't look back."

As they slowly continued trudging through the course rocks and up the edge of the mountain, the dead man's voice echoed in their ears, growing more and more faint as they pressed on, "Blood. Blood. Please. Need blood." Nes'egrinon told Kerlith to not look back.

Eventually they arrived at a small landing chipped into the side of the mountain. Alexius announced, "Here. We camp here. Tuck yourselves up against the side of the mountain and huddle together. Conserve your warmth."

It was bitterly cold and there was nothing to burn. They ate another portion of their rations but even had they eaten it all it would not have been enough.

Cautiously one of the soldiers left his group and stood in front of Kerlith and Bel. "It was good what you did back there. There is no dishonor in it. You cared for your master long after many a man would have left him. You cared for him even in his death. Do not worry for him. The dead take care of the dead."

Kerlith responded shallowly, "Thank you."

They thought the guard would leave, but he continued. "They call me Kephas. It means rock in our language, as you might suspect, a very common name here among the stonecutters. I had a brother. Perhaps you might know him? He would be about your age; he went to Lasaat about six years ago. We have not heard from him."

Bel replied, "What was his name?"

The soldier became less wary and more comfortable

with these two but he dared not let his eyes drift over to the archmage. "Petras. Hahaha. That also means rock. We have many, many names for all the different kinds of rocks here, you see. Kephas is a small, soft rock, more of a stone actually. Petras can be small or large, but they are usually jagged and hard. Like the ones we have been walking on all day. That was him; his name fit him. Did you know him?"

Kerlith answered first, "Petras? Yes, I knew of him. He was one year ahead of us. I saw him in the courts and practice fields. I never spoke to him though. I remember when he graduated. He went to the desert lands, I think."

Bel added, "Yes, that sounds right. He studied hard and worked hard. I guess his name did fit him."

Kephas sat down in front of them.

Kerlith said, "I always wondered who came from these lands for me to be sent here. My people are stonecutters also, but from the Midwestern mountains, very far from here. It was hard for me to leave them, especially since I did not know if I would be assigned to such a people when and if I graduated."

Bel added, "Kephas, you know how it works, don't you? Since your brother was called?"

"Somewhat. I was out on a mission when they came looking for him. When I returned home he was already gone. My kin said that our people would receive a mage if Petras completed his studies and graduated. We never heard from him again but some years later I had heard from the old women that Muolithnon had an apprentice. I cried that day for I knew Petras had made it."

Kerlith smiled. "Yes, that's what happened. I was so happy to be among the stonecutters again. We don't choose our assignments; they choose us and I loathed to go to the tundra or desert lands. I was blessed to have stone magic in my blood."

"Yes. That's how it was with my brother," the soldier said. "He always seemed extraordinarily good at things. Lucky, I always thought. But there was something deep inside of him, wasn't there?"

Bel replied, "That's the way it works. You have to be born to it. Predestined is the term they use at school, you know, you are either born with it or you're not."

"So how does it work?" the guard said innocently. Bel and Kerlith looked at each other, then over at the archmage who looked to be lost in deep thought.

"What do you mean?" Bel said.

"The words. You use magic words. I don't understand why a person has to be born into it if you are using magic words. Cannot anyone learn the words?"

Bel and Kerlith looked at each other once more then Nes'egrinon said softly, "Fifth Year, you can answer that one question but nothing more."

The guard tensed but refused to look over at the old wizard.

Bel started, "It's like this. When you speak, or I speak, or anyone speaks for that matter, we breathe in the air of the world and something in our throat vibrates as the air passes out and into another's ears. This is normal speech and all things that make noise or speak, whether they be of creature-kind or human-kind, do something like this. You understand this, do you not?"

"Yes, of course."

"Now a mage or an apprentice will speak like that also. But they also have learned another speech, a different speech, and it is not just learning a different language; it is the old language, the language of the ancients and it is much, much more than merely air vibrations from one's mouth to another's ears."

"What is it?"

Bel looked at his master who nodded. Bel said, "There is a saying at Lasaat that every First Year learns, 'Life and death is in the power of the tongue.' And what is truth is that this is not referring to the words that any human speaks but to mage-words, the words of power. You see, the word *tongue* has two meanings, one meaning is the body part in your mouth, the other is *language*. The saying refers to both of these. Life and death is in the power of the *tongue* and life and death is in the power of the *language*. You must have both and the language that is being referred to is not just a collection of mere words."

"I never heard this before."

"Yes. To your ears it sounds like normal speech, but it is not. In fact it is something much more, something unseen, something that is happening inside. What you may have observed when you heard us speak those words was the outward manifestation of something that was happening inside, internally, inside of our bodies. The people of the tundra lands call it ch'i. In other lands it is called a spirit and in still others it has no name. At Lasaat it is called life-force. Whatever it is, it has power and energy. When a wizard does his magic, something unseen is happening inside of him, deep down in his life-force, calling to the life around him, connecting with it, asking it to help him, to do what is needed to accomplish the task —"

"That's enough," Nes'egrinon said calmly and without malice. "We do not need to give away all of our secrets in one day. We must rest, young stonecutter."

Kephas arose and nodded then retreated to his friends.

Bel said, "Master, I do not understand. You allowed me tell him those things but then you stopped me when I started to speak."

He replied, "What do you mean you don't understand?"

When Bel did not answer but only stared dumbfounded, the wizard looked over at Kerlith. "You too?"

Kerlith said, "I'm not getting into this one," then rolled over.

"So, two knuckleheads. What were you planning to do, tell him everything? Then what? He tries to do something and kills someone. With my luck, it'd be me."

Bel tried to defend himself, "But Master, then why did you let me start?"

"I first let you speak so that he would understand that he should not try it himself, that there was more to it than what he had in his mind. I stopped you for the same reason. Too much information in the hands of the uninitiated can only lead to death. Remember what you just said—life and death is in the power of the tongue."

The mage exhaled then closed his eyes. Exhaustion showed on his face and they all slept quickly but it was fitful sleep. The three could not escape the pull they felt, the ominous dread calling to them, even in their rest. They all knew that they no longer needed Muolithnon to lead them. Bel thought he could find the breach blindfolded, the tug was so strong. But what they all feared was the unknown reason why the breach was pulling them toward it and who was behind the gnawing yearn to run headlong into whatever it had planned for them.

Chapter Thirteen
Hell Hounds

They were awakened by the sounds of barking in the distance, not knowing how long they had slept.

"Dogs? Here?" one soldier said.

Kephas replied, "It is as in the stories of old. The hounds of hell. We are close."

"Aye," Alexius breathed.

Another said morbidly, "It sounds as if there are many out there."

They quickly packed their bags and started back on the path, scaling the steep height. After a time they reached the summit and paused to drink the last of their water. They had no more supplies; the food was gone; the water was gone but they were not so troubled as no one still imagined that they would return from this journey.

Their eyes looked down upon the dark valley below and the large black rift at the far end of it.

Bel said, "Master, is that it?"

"What do you think? What does your spirit tell you?"

"I feel it calling to me. I think that it is the breach," Bel replied.

"What say you, apprentice?" Nes'egrinon said to Kerlith.

"The Fifth Year is right." Kerlith answered.

"I would appreciate it if you didn't call me that," Bel retorted as his eyes rolled.

"It's your name. Or would you prefer wiggle-farts?" Kerlith smiled.

"Enough!" Nes'egrinon barked. "You two may need each other soon. Start acting like it." He then pointed his finger off into the black. "Now that, right there, is the breach. How could it be anything else?" The old mage stared at it with a puzzled look on his face. Bel knew what he was thinking: Now what? How do we close it? How did it get there?

The barking grew closer and more distinct; there was more than one dog, that's for sure. And they would be on them soon.

Alexius told his men, "Ready your swords. Do not go down unarmed." He looked around at them and the doubt on their faces, and then continued, "Today is the day. We should reach the breach today. Lighten your loads. Drop anything that you do not need. There is a saying among the stonecutters, 'Live everyday as if it is your last.' Today we do that more than ever. Lighten your loads, my friends, and prepare yourselves."

The men had little weight to shed but a few things they refused to throw down, trinkets, keepsakes, mementos and the like. They pulled them out for a few moments, looking at them longingly; a bracelet of small stones made by a child, a polished stone in the shape of a heart, a simple bracelet of twine that had an unknown memory attached to it.

Bel and Kerlith watched them but had no such things; they had forsaken everything to become wizards and all that they carried of their previous lives resided in their minds.

The barking grew louder and looking down the mountain into the valley they could now see motion in the darkness. The dogs were coming.

"Prepare yourselves!" Nes'egrinon hollered.

The soldiers tightened their grips on their swords; Kerlith gripped his stone; Bel and Nes'egrinon their staffs; the three men of magic called light to enter their implements.

"There! There!" Kephas said, pointing at the motion down below and to the right.

Another soldier yelled, "There's another! And another! Two over here on the left! Coming in fast!"

Alexius, up in front, hollered, "Hold! Hold! Wait for it! Hold the line!" Several dogs bounded straight up the middle at them, barking excitedly.

Bel held power in his staff, it pulsating with life-energy, like an extension of his own body, his own life-force pushed out into the end of the glowing piece of mage-wood.

The dogs did not stop and snarl or bark when they reached them but continued their full speed run into a leap, mouths open, teeth glistening, sharp nails of their paws reaching out to strike.

Kerlith and Bel yelped, "Apokrothos!" simultaneously, each repelling one of the oversized black dogs down the mountain. They fell onto the jagged rocks and tumbled down the sheer cliff edge. Another one of the hounds sprung from the left onto two of the soldiers, both swinging their swords. One missed and the dog chomped on his arm, him screaming terribly as the bones of his forearm snapped. The other struck home, his sword landing deep in the beast's neck, impaling himself on the sword as his heavy weight pinned the two men down. The dog was larger than both of the two men combined, a giant hound of Hell.

Bel and Kerlith ran to their aid, their eyes darting around them as Nes'egrinon banished dog after dog, and Alexius and Kephas faced down the animals from the front. Kerlith paralyzed the huge dog with his magic and the two boys rolled it off of the men, the dog not able to resist them with anything more than a guttural growl.

The two men stood up and one began sawing the dead dog's head off, much as they did the ghoul-kind they fought at the Keep of the stonecutters. The other winced as he tucked his broken arm into his jacket and put his sword in his other hand; sweat mixed with tears on his grimy face.

Bel and Kerlith spun and leapt to Kephas' aid as another dog dove toward him. The soldier parried with his sword, quickly slicing off one of the beast's legs, it landing behind him, the dog whimpering for a moment then snarling with rage. Bel blasted the hound into the air and down the mountain.

The old mage looked back at him and frowned, quickly saying, "Not so hard! Don't use so much energy!"

Three dogs bounded up the mountain at them from the front. Nes'egrinon touched his staff on the back of a large boulder, light slithering out of the end of his stick of mage-wood and spreading into the large rock threadlike, spiraling across the hard surface in small ringlets of power and light.

The boulder struggled to move from its perch, then rolled slowly, then more quickly, gaining speed, tumbling down the mountain, hitting others on the way, creating a small landslide, unavoidable by the approaching dogs. The animals tried to dodge but were pulled under the bouncing rocks.

The band looked about, here and there for others but the silence told them that they were all gone.

Kerlith smiled and said, "Was that stone magic, Master Archmage?"

"My hand never left my staff. I am a mage of the wood, not a heretic like Rylith who attempts to control all life," he said shortly, clearly not liking the boy's questioning attitude.

Alexius said, "Report! Are any injured?"

The soldier who was bitten heaved, saying, "I'm sorry, my commander. The hound got my good arm. I can still fight though." But everyone knew that he lied. He would not last long at all. His blood was everywhere.

Alexius gingerly slid the man's arm out to see a mangled, bloody and broken piece of flesh, skin torn to ribbons, fibers and bone fragments exposed below. He said out loud, refusing to look the man in the eyes just yet, "Master Archmage, can you do anything?"

"I can. I can dull the pain. But that's about it right now. In this place."

"Do it! Do it, please!" the man said, suddenly nearly in tears as he looked down at his arm.

Alexius slid the arm back into the man's shirt then tied a piece of cloth to support its weight as Nes'egrinon placed his hand on the man's head and pushed from deep within himself. The man exhaled slowly as relief poured into him.

The band did not speak as they began to descend the mountain, all somehow knowing that they shared a common fate with the man whose arm was destroyed. They trudged down for a time, going long past when they would have stopped for a few moments to take in some dry crusts or seasoned meats but they had no supplies left, not even water, so they continued on without stopping, all of their mouths growing more and more parched.

As they carefully stepped from stone to stone and rock to rock, Bel felt his mind drawn to the battle with the dogs. Kerlith and I used the same magic yet his seemed so much stronger. I know we are in the land of the stonecutters and his magic should be a bit more effective, but it was much more than that. I wish I hadn't gotten stuck in Lasaat for that sixth year. A mix of jealousy and resentment grabbed Bel's heart. He didn't flee from the responsibility of the challenge that trapped him in Lasaat and prevented him from moving on, but he also recognized Kerlith's guilt. And now the one partially to blame for his setback had gained a year of private instruction, a year that Bel didn't have, and it appeared that Kerlith's magic was far more refined than his. Maybe I am only a Fifth Year, Bel thought, suddenly despising himself.

"Fifth Year," Nes'egrinon's voice rang out in the black, shaking Bel from his thoughts, "guard your mind. Kerlith, you too. Something is close. Something is here, trying to invade our thoughts. Do you feel it?"

Kerlith choked, "I feel it."

When Bel did not immediately respond, the old man said, "Fifth Year, what were you thinking?"

"I… nothing."

"Listen. Do not trust your thoughts right now if they would divide us. Don't listen to the enemy. He's here, somewhere, among us."

"Yes, Master," Bel replied but something gnawed at him in his thoughts. Whatever the source of these thoughts does not matter, Bel pondered, even if they're from the enemy, they are still true. My magic is weak. I'm just a Fifth Year. What am I even doing here? I'm going to get myself killed. I'm going to get some of these men killed. I can't do this! I shouldn't be here!

Nes'egrinon stopped, holding his hand high. "Wait," he said. They all looked about, straining their ears but all was black and silent, all except the faraway groan of a dead dog's head severed from its body that they left back high up on the mountain in what now seemed like ages ago. "Something. Something's here."

A tear streamed down Bel's cheeks as he squealed, "I can't do this! I can't! I'm only a Fifth Year!" then crumbled to the floor, his short staff falling to the ground in front of him.

Nes'egrinon dashed over to him, "No! Get him out of

your head! Fight it! Fight! You can do it, boy!"

Bel refused to look up, blubbering, "You're lying! Just like you did before. He told me! He told me you would!"

"Who?" said Kerlith, "Who are you talking about?" His voice trembled.

Bel looked up at Kerlith, suddenly feeling tremendously inferior to him, "My Master has had only two apprentices before me. He killed them both. Everyone knows it!"

Nes'egrinon's face grew dark. Bel continued, now looking at his master full in the face, "He came to me. One of them. He told me. He told me that you lied to him! He told me what you did! You got him killed!"

"No..." the old mage said, stumbling back a few steps.

Bel's accusations grew stronger, "He told me and I saw it! I saw his arm. It was blown clean off! Just a burnt stump where a boy's arm should have been. And he was so young! How long did you teach him before he died? He was younger than me! And now I'm fresh out of school and you're so quickly leading me to my death? And all of us too?"

Kerlith and the soldiers looked at the panic on Nes'egrinon's face then at the pain on Bel's, then at the ground and away. None of them could stand to look at it. Reality; it was reality; it was the reality that they couldn't last more than another half day or so. And for what? They followed an old wizard with no plan and with no clue what they were even up against. They didn't have enough supplies. They were ill prepared and ill advised. It was a doomed mission from the start. One of the soldiers began to mutter to Kephas. He wanted to leave. He suddenly wanted to leave right now, to run, right now. Despair and anguish hung thick in the air.

The man with the broken arm began to sob loudly then howled, "We're all going to die! Now! Now! Death is upon us! We're going to die now!"

"Quiet soldier! Grab a hold of yourself!" Alexius huffed, but it was no use; he felt it too. He was the chief of guards and he had left his post to die in the black. He didn't belong here. He belonged at the Keep, where he could do some good, where he could lead his men to victory against the ghoul-kind, where he could protect his people. He had abandoned his people. Out here, he was a dead man walking. He didn't belong here and he wanted to run and run and run. He wanted to flee from this place with all of his might. He was afraid.

Kerlith howled out in pain, "It was all my fault! My master is dead! I should have stopped them! I should have cast the love spell but I didn't and now he's dead! Then I left him there like old trash to wander in the black! I don't deserve to live!"

The soldiers began beating their breasts and crying loudly for they had left their children fatherless and their wives would soon be widows. One tore at his clothing and another ran in circles screaming. Alexius threw down his sword and howled, "I'm not fit to lead! I'm a failure!"

"Stop." Nes'egrinon squeezed his eyes down tight. "Stop. Stop. Stop! STOP!" The old mage lifted his staff high and desperately pushed bright light into it not knowing what else to do, "Phos! Phos! Phos!"

The sky lit up brightly in hazy greens and blues, shining full of unnatural mage-light and about ten paces away stood a small, frail boy, staring at them, grinning intently, his ragged, dirty and torn clothing the color of a urine-stained sun, a short mage-wood staff in one hand and a blood caked flask hanging from his shoulder, a young child of a man, a boy with only one arm, grinning wildly.

Chapter Fourteen

Fleck

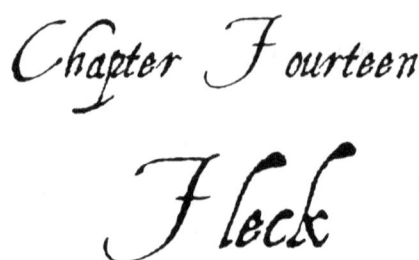

"How did you like my dogs? I've been training them for some time," The one-armed boy said.

The band slowly walked towards the boy, fanning out in a sort of arc around him, the soldiers with their swords nervously drawn, each realizing that the boy was somehow in their minds. As the mage-light overhead began to fade, Kerlith wiped his face then called light into the surrounding stones, the tiny chips of crystal and quartz in each of the rocks glowing brightly, casting a dim light up from the ground at the boy's face. The one-armed boy turned as they approached, keeping his stump of a missing arm behind him.

"What have you done, Fleck? Why?" Nes'egrinon asked.

"Fleck? Hmm. Yes, that was my name wasn't it? I had forgotten. How long have I been dead? Looking at the age on your face it must have been at least thirty years. We have no time in the underworld, you know. One day or one hundred, it is all the same. It feels as if it is one continuous moment. But fortunately for me I had my dogs. And I trained them. You didn't tell me. How did you like them?"

The band was a short distance from the boy and they halted their approach. They each tried to shake the feeling that still grabbed them: fear, dread, the desire to run away, far, far away from this place. The feeling was still there and even though they each knew that it was a false feeling, a sensation pushed into their minds by the dead boy, it felt no less real than any other feeling that they had ever had. It was difficult to overcome.

The old man continued to address him. "Fleck. You are insane, aren't you? Why did you set the dogs upon us?"

"Why? Why not? All of you will soon be dead anyway. What does a few more moments of life for you or your men matter to me? Anyway, these others I have no quarrel with. I just wanted to see how my dogs would do."

"And me? You have a quarrel with me then."

The boy suddenly hissed, "You know I do!" He pulled his head back and smiled mischievously then drank from his flask and wiped his bloody mouth.

The mage looked over at Kerlith and Bel and nodded

then continued speaking, "Listen son, I'm sorry for what happened. You know that I am. I labored over your death for years. How many years has it been you asked? Yes, thirty, perhaps more than thirty, and only now have I taken on a new apprentice. In the moment of your death I would have traded places with you in an instant. But who can cheat death?"

Bel and Kerlith continued to move slowly, inching behind the boy. Bel shook his head a few times; he was so dizzy, tired and worn out; the fight with the dogs took more out of him than he had realized.

The boy smiled again. "No one can cheat death. Enough of these words, we will have much time to talk when you join me here in the underworld. All of you who surround me, leave this fight. It is between the two of us alone. If you would value your lives you will stay out of my way." He took one more swig from his flask, a shudder passed through him and the hairs on his head began to glow brightly, greens and blues emanating from each hair like glowing tendrils waving in the air.

The old mage sounded suddenly desperate. "Fleck, please. Leave off from this madness. You were my apprentice and I'm sorry that you died but if you challenge me I will have to destroy you."

"Destroy me? You cannot harm me. You can't kill me. I'm already dead, remember?" The boy pointed his staff at the old man and squeezed. A large ball of light erupted from the end of it and arced out toward the old man who quickly lifted up his own staff sideways. The round orb of light struck the stick of mage-wood, knocking the mage back a few steps, him gasping loudly under the force, then the light dissipated into his staff.

The boy laughed loudly, arching his back and tilting his head toward the black sky, "Hahaha. How weak have you become, old man? When I was your apprentice you would have swatted that away with the flick of your wrist."

Kerlith and Bel were now behind the boy. Bel couldn't stop staring at the burnt hole in the boy's body, the empty socket where his arm should have been. He was mesmerized by it and was having trouble focusing on anything else; a fog was in his mind. The soldiers still stood to the mage's left, swords drawn, but their enemy ignored them as if they were insignificant as buzzing flies.

Nes'egrinon spoke, "Listen, I don't want to fight you. You know this. For... for I love you. But if you continue then I will unleash a force that even a ghoul-mage cannot withstand."

A puzzled look stole over Bel's face. Something was not right here but he couldn't seem to figure it out; he couldn't seem to think.

"Fine. Don't fight back and die or fight back and die. It makes no difference to me," the boy howled as he sent another blast towards the mage, then another, then another, then another. Each time the archmage held up his staff in defense, absorbing the light, absorbing the power. It knocked him back further each time and after the last blast he found himself down on one knee, his right hand bracing his body on a boulder, trying to hold back the successive onslaught of deadly energy.

"What? Is that all you are going to do? Let me pummel you? You owe me a fight!"

Nes'egrinon slammed his staff into the ground then used it to pull himself up to his feet. He twisted the staff in the ground softly as he stood and breathed hard, huffing air. "You're right, I'm old. I can't stand much more of this. I ask mercy of you. We're on a journey to close this breach. If you would have my life once our mission is complete then I'll give it to you gladly. I'll join you in the underworld."

"Hahaha. Close the breach. Impossible. How do you think this breach came to be anyway?"

Tiny roots clawed their way from among the stones and rocks littered on the ground as the old mage continued to gently twist his staff. They wrapped themselves around Fleck's feet, ankles and legs.

Fleck spoke excitedly, "I did it! I caused the breach to rip open! I poisoned his mind. Called to him for years!" He bellowed, proud of himself, "The others said it couldn't be done. The other dead mages, fools all, said that the dead could not communicate with the living. But they forgot about dreams! Dreams, dreams, wonderful, terrible dreams! I got into them. All I needed to do was find a mind that was so full of the hope and lust for glory that he would believe almost anything to get it, the mind of a mage, one who could actually do something to set me free. I found him and entered his dreams. It took time, probably at least twenty years, but what was time to me?"

The tendrils were wrapped around the boy's legs up to the knees now.

"It is I who did this, Father. That's right! All of you have heard me say it. This man who stands before you, this so-called great mage, he is my father and it is because of him that I am dead and because of him that this breach is open! The very fabric of reality has been torn asunder and you have him to blame! I tell you this, you will join me, Father mine. But it will not be a happy reunion."

Nes'egrinon screamed, "Now!" as he lifted then swung his staff down at the boy, pushing out all of the energy that he had been absorbing and holding. A giant flash of energy exploded out of his staff toward the one-armed boy. Kerlith and Bel each pointed at the boy from behind, attacking him with magic and the soldiers leapt at him with their swords.

The boy tried to quickly kneel into a defensive position but his lower legs were held tight and he began to lose his balance, flailing his single arm. He quickly formed a barrier of protection around himself, a thin blue orb of energy, as he tumbled. The soldiers were rebuffed when they struck the orb but Nes'egrinon's attack pierced it, disintegrating the shield. The boy fell back, landing hard on the ground and Bel poured all he had into one last ball of magic, speaking in the old tongue, "Baru! Baru! Baru!" calling a massive increase in the density of the boy's limbs. They became so heavy that he could not lift them. Even his head fell to the side and his tongue out of his mouth, lying on the earth, so heavy that he could not lift it to speak. The force of energy drained Bel so deeply that he could barely stand. Bel felt incoherent; he knew he was fading but he couldn't stop; he had to see this through.

The archmage stood over his son and said, "My son, I'm sorry. I am truly sorry. I didn't mean for things to happen as they have but dead or not you are still my son and you need a spanking."

Bel and Kerlith looked at the old man, their eyes changed, their opinion and knowledge of the old man now broken. The old man was not who they thought he was. He had a son, secretly. All wizards, upon graduating from Lasaat took the oath to not marry or have children. Now here stood a wizard who not only had a son, but also somehow got him into Lasaat without the other masters knowing who the boy's father was, then—and this was incredible—got his own son assigned to him as apprentice. The gears in their minds spun feverishly. To do all of that and then for the boy to die? That must have ripped the old man apart. No wonder he hadn't taken an apprentice until now.

Dizziness spun Bel around and around and he realized that the spell drained him further than he thought. He reached out, grabbing Kerlith's shoulder to steady himself.

The archmage spoke, "My son, now we will go on. If we fail then perhaps I will be joining you this day. If not and we succeed then it will not be long. I'm old and have not much life left in me. I'll join you, whether it is this day or another. We'll speak and you will know my heart. I hope that one day you will forgive me for your death." The old mage spoke to the others, "Come. We must go. Bel, Kerlith, drain him."

Bel said, "What?" in a sort of a daze.

"You heard me. Drain his energy. We need it. You can't kill him. Go ahead. Do it."

Kerlith looked at Bel and said, "Now this is a new one. Draining energy from the dead?"

They knew all living creatures had life—that was common sense—and magic was merely a manipulation of that life, but to draw life from what was dead? Something just didn't sound right about it. Kerlith placed his hand on the immobilized boy and pulled in his spirit. He felt energy so he drew on it more, pulling it into himself. Bel stood back and watched, unsure.

Fleck began to laugh, a hideous, gurgling sort of laugh, as his tongue and his mouth were not under his control.

Bel grabbed at Kerlith's shoulder, nearly ready to fall over. "Are you sure? How does it feel?"

Fleck's eyes rolled to the outer edge of their sockets and stared up at Bel. He continued to laugh, sucking dust and dirt into his mouth.

"I feel energy. I feel life. But it is... tainted." Kerlith was initially cautious but then smiled oddly and pulled hard.

The one-armed boy squealed in pain as the color drained from his skin and faded to a deep, dark gray. Kerlith removed his hand from the dead boy whose eyes stared forward vacantly, mouth mumbling, "Bloo. Bloo-da. Nee bloo-da," unable to properly form the words.

Kerlith said, "It feels weird. It is energy, yes, but I am not sure if that was such a good idea."

The archmage stood tall. "One last thing, Fleck. If you try this kind of stunt when I am dead, I'll give you a spanking there too. Okay everyone, there is little time. We must go now while we still can."

Bel teetered then fell over.

Kerlith said, "Hey, stop fooling around. Oh. Master Archmage, I think your Fifth Year here passed out."

Alexius and Kephas went to the two men who lay on the ground unmoving. Alexius spoke first, "Wait a moment Master Archmage. I think these two have joined the dead." Alexius pushed on one of their shoulders with his boot.

One of the freshly dead men began to stir. He coughed a few times then opened his eyes and wiped the dirt from his mouth. He looked up at Alexius then over to Nes'egrinon then sat up. He pulled his arm out of his jacket. "Even in death, my arm is still damaged. It no longer bleeds though. Uhhh, my head really hurts. My chief, oh my chief. Alexius, I have failed you. Please tell my dear Bella that I love her. Please tell her that I fought well. Oh, it is coming. I feel my mind slipping. It is growing hazy. Please, help me stand."

Alexius lent his arm to his fallen comrade and as he did the other dead man began to stir. Meanwhile, in the distance, the boy with one arm could not stop laughing. The other dead soldier's eyes snapped open. "What? What happened? My head hurts. Man, oh man." He reached back and felt the back of his head. "I think I busted my head. Hey Alexius, could you help me up?"

Alexius helped the second man up to a seated position. He squatted down on his knees and looked at him eye level. "How do you feel?"

"Pretty good. My head is pounding. Real hungry too. Man I could use something to drink." The man's eyes popped open wide. "Hey, I'm not dead, am I?"

Kephas said, "Do you feel dead?"

"No. I feel pretty alive. Except... the idea of drinking some blood just popped into my head and... Awww man! I *am* dead!"

"I am sorry, friend." Alexius stood and held out his hand.

"Get that thing away from me! I'm dead! Thanks a lot!" The dead man stood and rubbed the gash on the back of his head. "You know, just a few minutes ago, when that one-armed nut job came around I was really thinking seriously about getting out of here. I was going to run away. Yeah, that's it. Run away all the way back to the Keep. But nooooo. I had to stay and help. Now I'm dead."

The other dead man said, "Don't be upset. Everyone dies. Let us go on together."

"With you? I don't even like you. There. I said it. We have been serving on the same guard for almost four years and I never told you. You know why? You fart too much in the guard shack. I mean, what's with that? You see me there and then you fart. And what's worse is that you aim that cannon toward me first. Hey this is not target practice, you know."

"I'm sorry. You should have said something."

"Said something? Are you kidding me? What should I have said? Excuse me, please don't fart when my mouth is open? C'mon! No one has to be told that. And they stunk too. What were you eating? Dead carcass sandwich smothered in sewage stained underwear? And hey, did I say my mouth was open? Yuck! No way am I going anywhere with you and that stench cannon you're carrying around."

The first soldier turned to leave, saying, "I must go. I must go from here before the desire for blood overtakes me." The soldier stumbled off into the darkness.

The other said, "Yeah. Get out of here, stinky. Alexius, I am not happy about this. But, well, what can I do? I am going the other way. I don't want to bump into stinky out there in the dark. You never know what he's going to smell like now that's he's dead. I mean, he smelled dead when he was alive. Can you imagine what he's going to smell like now? Oh well, I'm leaving."

Nes'egrinon slapped Bel on the face, trying to wake him but he was too far drained, he had given too much of his life-force. He was alive, but close to death.

Kephas said, "If I may make a suggestion? I will stay here with the boy and watch him. He seems to be too far-gone to be of any use to you. Am I right? If he regains consciousness and seems able we will follow after you. And while I am here I can keep an eye on your dead son there too."

The archmage rubbed his scar and said, "Hmm. I don't like it but it looks as if I have no choice. Yes, you stay here with him. We will go on and see what we will see. So soon and we are down to three."

Chapter Fifteen

Valley Of Death

"What? Where am I?" Bel said as he tried to look around in the blackness. He couldn't see anything. Somewhere nearby he heard some scuffling and a voice mumbling something about blood. The ghoul-kind! They are close! Keep quiet!

Bel tried to shake the fog from his mind. He felt extremely tired and he had no idea how long he was out. The last he remembered they were just over the peak of a large mountain staring down into a valley and... the breach. Yes, the breach.

"I remember now," he whispered to himself. We saw the breach, at least what we thought was the breach. It looked like a large tear. Unnatural. That had to be it. Then... dogs! The dogs attacked then the one-armed boy from my dreams. I think we defeated him. But Bel wasn't so sure. He couldn't remember much about that battle. He said he was Master's son! Master Nes'egrinon had a son! It became more incredible the more Bel dwelled on it. I wonder if any of the other mage-kind has secret lives and secret children. This changed everything. The world of magic was revealing itself more and more to be not what Bel thought, not what he was taught in school.

"Hey! You're awake!" Kephas stood over Bel, holding a small torch.

"Kephas, what happened? Where am I?"

"How much do you remember?"

"We were fighting the boy with one-arm."

Kephas glanced back. "He's over there. It was tough, but we overcame him. It cost us much though. Two of my friends are dead. And you, well, you passed out afterward."

"I did?"

Kephas squatted next to the boy. "Yes, I think you drained yourself too much. At least that's what I overheard the archmage say as they left."

"Left! They went on without me?"

"Yes."

"Help me up!"

Kephas grabbed Bel's arm and hoisted him up into a seated position. "I promised him I would look after you. You were unconscious. Do you think you are strong enough to go on?"

Bel could hear the calls for blood nearby. "I don't know but—" Bel cut his words short; he was still very dizzy. He didn't like the idea of going down there and now he had an excuse not to. And it wasn't some lame, schoolboy excuse made up to get out of taking an exam; he passed out; it was a totally valid excuse to not go down into the valley and die. It was so very tempting to just lie back down and fall asleep but Bel knew he couldn't do that. Nes'egrinon was *his* master; he had to go help him. "I think I can make it. Please, help me up. Which way did they go?"

"Bloo-da! Nee-da bloo-da! Hahahaha!" the one-arm boy shrieked loudly.

"Shut up over there!" Kephas yelled as he hoisted Bel up off the ground. He kept one hand on his arm, as he did not know if the boy could stand on his own. The dim torchlight flickered. "Listen, I don't think that's a good idea. You are too weak."

"I'll be fine. I promise. I need to go help them. They need me. They do. They need…" Bel teetered.

"Woah there. Okay, let's sit back down." The soldier eased Bel back to the ground and stared at his soft boyish face. "You know you look a bit like Petras. I imagine at his age he might look like you."

Bel did not respond. He was finding it difficult to keep his eyes open at the moment.

"Tell you what. You can take some of my energy. Like

your friend did to the dead boy over there. Just don't take too much. I mean, don't drain me dead; don't kill me. Oh boy, am I really going to do this? Alright, listen. Are you in there? Hello? Wake up." He shook Bel then shook him again.

He opened his eyes slowly, "Hey, Kephas, I need to go help—"

The guard placed his hand on Bel's chest and said, "Take it. Take some of my energy."

Bel didn't do it consciously; he didn't even know how it happened or why; he didn't even know it was happening at all. Perhaps it was the thirst for life, the same thirst that the ghoul-kind had, that caused him to drink in Kephas' life-force, draining the light out of him. Perhaps it was the desire that all living things have to live life, even if it is just for a few moments longer. Bel had once seen a cat catch a bird. Clearly the bird would die; it was in the mouth of the cat and its wings were broken. Even had the cat dropped it there on the ground, the bird would die soon. Yet it struggled on. Did it not know that it would soon die? Yet it struggled because a few more moments of life, even in the mouth of a cat, were better than the darkness of death. Bel unconsciously drank deeply.

Suddenly Bel felt strong, aware and awake, more alive than he had felt in days. He felt full of light, full of energy. He looked down at his arms and they almost glistened. There was a torch lying on the ground next to him so he picked it up and looked around. Next to him lay Kephas. What's this! What had he done?

Bel shook him and he did not move. A grim foreboding grabbed Bel in the pit of his stomach. What. Had. He. Done?! Bel shook Kephas harder this time.

"Nee-da bloo-da! Hahahaha!" rang out in the silent black.

"Shut up over there!" Bel screamed in a panic as he shook the soldier more and more vigorously. "Don't be dead. Please don't be dead."

"Bloo-da! Bloo-da!"

Bel tried to ignore the one-armed boy's cries. Perhaps he would be quiet if no one paid him any attention. Bel shook Kephas harder then sat back and stared at his body laying prostrate on the dirt, Kephas' arms and legs in a seemingly uncomfortable position draped over sharp rocks jutting out of the earth. The torch between them was almost out.

Bel choked back a sob. What have I done? he thought.

"Bloo-da!"

Bel stood quickly, grabbed the torch and ran over toward the sound. He looked down at the boy and kicked him square in the back. "This is all your fault!"

"Bloo-da! Nee-da bloo-da!"

"Shut up. Shut up. Shut up!" Bel hated hearing those cries for blood because he suddenly felt no better than him. He needed life so he drained Kephas; he drained him dry. He didn't mean to do it. He didn't even know that he was doing it, yet he did it just the same. He was no better than one of these dead ghouls crying out for blood. They were merely articulating their desire a little more obviously, a little more grotesquely, but they were all the same, predators, feeding on each other in one giant game of who can consume whom first. It was that stupid idea they taught the First Years, the great circle of life, but suddenly it didn't seem so great and Bel was disgusted with himself. He felt like throwing up but he knew his belly had been too empty to do that for a long time now.

"Bloo-da!"

"Shut up, I said!" Bel kicked the boy again, harder this time.

"Hahahaha!"

"Shut it! Just shut it!" Bel kicked him a few more times but then stopped. It did no good. He retreated to Kephas' prone body and sat next to him. "Why? Why'd you do it? You could have left me here. You could have lived."

Then Bel saw the most amazing thing. Kephas little finger moved! It was a tiny move, the tiniest of moves, but still, it moved! Bel hunched over him, placing the side of his face just over Kephas mouth, trying to see if he could feel his breath on his cheek. He couldn't feel anything. I saw his finger move didn't I? He must be still alive; he must be! Bel put his hand on his chest and pushed a little life into him, saying the mage words of healing. He stopped and waited, hoping against hope that the soldier was still with the living.

Kephas said shallowly, "You're still here?"

"I don't want you to die. Please. I can't be like them."

The soldier pondered the words, not understanding what the boy meant by them. He was just a simple man, a guard of the Keep of the stonecutters and he did not grasp their meaning. "You must go on. You must help them to close the gateway."

"I can't go. Not until I know that you will be alright, not until I know that you aren't going to die out here."

"Please. Go. I'll be fine. I am awake. See? Just go. Go now."

Bel wiped his face, unsure whether or not there might be a trace of moisture on his cheek. He stood and looked down at the soldier and said, "Are you sure?"

"Yes. I'm fine. I feel better already." But the soldier lied. The echoes of laughter coming from the one-armed boy rang in his ears as he lied. He was not fine. In fact, he was not even alive. He had joined the dead. He was one of the ghoul-kind. But for all his strength and fearlessness in battle he did not have the courage to tell the boy who so looked like his younger brother.

Bel wanted to believe him. He needed to believe him although in his spirit he knew his words were false. He turned his head and looked down at the breach then back once more. "Okay then. I am going to go help them. As long as you are alright."

"I'm fine. Go, please go."

It was then that Bel truly realized what had happened. He could not look at Kephas anymore, so he quickly turned, not saying another word, and started his journey down the mountain, down into the valley of death.

*****

Down in the valley, Nes'egrinon, Alexius and Kerlith were near the base of the mountain. The slope was leveling out and there were ghoul-kind milling about everywhere. Some asked them for blood but they were mostly the calm type and did not attack. Many wore clothing that Kerlith had never seen before. A few items reminded him of something that he had heard his history teacher describe, at least what he imagined that it would look like, the clothing of peoples from the forgotten times, many, many generations past. Most of them that asked for blood spoke in an unintelligible speech, some in languages that almost didn't seem as if they could be languages, clicks, snaps and beeps. But they knew what the dead were saying; they knew what they were asking for. Up ahead the crowds thickened and the three quickly realized that they would have to wade through hundreds, if not thousands of the ghoul-kind to reach the entrance.

Nes'egrinon said, "Alexius, Kerlith, gather round."

The old wizard grabbed their hands and slowly chanted in the old tongue, "Aoratos, aoratos, aoratos, aoratos." It was something Kerlith had never heard before. He did not know what would happen. Then, as he looked about, trying to understand what the magic would do, the old man began to fade. "Aoratos, aoratos, aoratos, aoratos." He was disappearing! Kerlith looked over at Alexius and Alexius was looking back except he was fading too.

Kerlith said, "You two are disappearing. What manner of magic is this?"

Alexius said, "You too. I can still feel your hand but I can't see you anymore. You're gone!"

"Quiet you two," Nes'egrinon said. "Obviously it's invisibility magic. Don't have to be a genius to figure that out. Something you stone heads never seen before, ehh? That's because it's not stone magic. Anyway, stick close. Don't get lost. They can't see us but we can't see each other either."

The mage placed Alexius' hand on his shoulder and Kerlith's hand on Alexius' shoulder and began wading through the sea of dead. He sometimes had to push them out of the way with his staff but they tended not to mind too much. The closer they came to the breach, the thicker the throng of ghoul-kind and the more they had to plow through, pushing the dead bodies out of the way more and more forcefully.

Even though Kerlith had his hand on the archmage's shoulder and he could feel Alexius' hand on his, he felt like he needed to speak, if for no other reason to at least hear his own voice, to remind himself that he was actually there. It was too surreal. He had often imagined the dead as ghosts, that's the way many of the stories went anyway. They called them shades or shadows, but here they were, in the middle of them, and the dead were more substantial than the living. Kerlith could not see himself and he felt more and more like a ghost and saw the dead more and more as the living.

"Master Archmage?"

"Shhh."

Kerlith whispered lower, "I'm sorry but I have to ask."

"Can't you keep quiet? What is it?"

The apprentice asked, "I thought we would have come across the other masters by now. Master Rylithnon and his companions."

"And do you think I know something about that?"

"I don't know. I just thought, yes, I thought you might know something."

"Well, I don't. I guess we're on our own. Maybe they took a different route. Maybe we were lied to. Maybe they ran like chickens and hightailed it out of here and there's not even the sign of their yellow tail feathers. I don't know.

Does it look like I got this all figured out?"

Kerlith was quiet. A few moments later Alexius spoke, "I saw them at the Keep. The Master Archmage Rylithnon. I lead him in to see King Luthgar, some number of days before you showed up."

Nes'egrinon pushed another group of ghoul-kind out of the way and they found themselves in a small clearing. "Anything else you want to share now that we are here surrounded by a thousand blood thirsty ghouls?"

"I think our king told you that the wizard passed through, headed into this valley."

"He did."

"He traveled with a few companions but I'm not sure whether they were magicians or not. I think they were porters that he may have hired. If they were mage-kind then I couldn't tell as they performed no magic and did not dress as one of the mage-kind does. Rylithnon was the only one who performed any magic at the Keep."

Kerlith said, "So he had a few days head start?"

Alexius answered, "I don't know how many days. It didn't seem important at the time. He was just another courtly visitor at Protolith. We used to get many. It was before the sky went black, that much I am sure of."

"What?" Nes'egrinon gasped.

"Shhh," Kerlith and Alexius hissed. Some of the ghoul-kind spun and began walking blindly in their direction. The archmage pulled the group to and fro in the small clearing, ensuring that the ghouls did not accidentally stumble into them.

The mage huffed, "The king didn't tell me that. At least not to my understanding. I thought Rylithnon came here to stop this. Now it appears that he may have been involved in starting it."

Kerlith and Alexius couldn't see the old man's scarred face but if they could they would have seen a face crowned in worry. Kerlith began to wonder if nothing among the mage-kind was as it seemed. No wonder Master Nes'egrinon always seemed so jaded and kept himself hid away in the forest and separate from the rest of the great wizards. He probably hated himself for what happened to his son, his own flesh and blood, but there was more to it than that. The way he disrespected the other wizards, even my own master, it was as if he thought their motives were impure, tainted and maybe even selfish. And maybe he has a right to think that way.

Kerlith said, "If it is true that Master Rylithnon started this, then why are not more wizards here to stop it? Why is it only us?" His voice sounded more and more ethereal to himself the longer he stayed invisible.

"This is the hard reality of things, young apprentice. Now you see magic for what it truly is. They probably taught you that we are all guardians of the truth and keepers of the peace, that we are somehow supposed to keep the world of men safe and good and right and normal. That's what they sold you on, right?"

Kerlith nodded even though he knew the archmage could not see him.

"Well guess what? A mage is only a human that knows the ways of magic. There's nothing special or sacred about him at all. He's just as human as anyone else; he can make mistakes, fall on his face, lie, cheat, steal, any of it—and guess what else? —all of it. Listen. I've been around a long time. Some would say too long."

The mage paused to move them around a block of wandering ghoul-kind then continued, "And I've seen a little too much. Maybe a lot too much. I can tell you right now that no one is coming. That's just the way it is. Okay, I said it. We are on our own because the rest of them are cowering in their little empires of snow and desert and stone and wood and they're there hiding. They're hiding in their beds with the covers pulled over their heads, hoping someone else takes care of this. How do I know this? Well let's just say that it's just the way people generally are. Let's leave it at that."

Kerlith was becoming upset. "I would never do that. My master either. He was the one who called you and you didn't want to come, remember?"

"You're right. I never said I was any different either. Don't think that I am. I'm no better than anyone else. Wait a few years; you'll get there too. Believe me I didn't start out this way, but we all get there eventually. Hey, enough about this anyway. If you live through this, you'll see."

Kerlith couldn't accept the archmage's depressing view of humanity but he had no further counterpoint so he said in defeat, "Well, you're here now."

"Yes, I am. And I'm going to close this breach or die trying but don't expect anyone to come help us. We're on our own out here. I'm sorry, kid."

Alexius said, "Master Nes'egrinon, there's some movement over there. It looks as if it may be something? Shall we investigate?"

The archmage growled, "Let's get this over with."

Chapter Sixteen

The Breach

Bel scuttled down the mountain as fast as he could, trying not to stumble over rocks and stones as he ran, leaping over small boulders, holding his staff long in front of him, mage-light shining brightly. The slope of the earth flattened and he barreled into the rambling mass of dead at the base of the mountain, pushing through them, him trying to not think about how crazy this all was.

The dead stepped out of his pathway, at least the ones that saw him coming, many reaching a hand out and touching his clothing or his skin as he dashed by, somehow pleased to at least touch the living.

Their dress was odd. These must have been dead a long, long time. Bel thought. No wonder they do not venture out much further. They have been dead too long.

Maybe they have forgotten what it feels like to be alive. Whatever the reason, Bel was glad that they did not try to attack him.

As they got thick in front of him his run quickly slowed to a jog then to a walk then to a slog as he had to push more and more of them out of the way.

The thickness of the presence of death wrapped around Bel, blanketing him in intense claustrophobia; he had to keep moving, had to keep pushing through or he would scream; he had to hold on; he could not let it escape his throat. They were everywhere! The deeper he got in, the more hands that reached out to touch him.

Now some saw him as he approached and waited, outstretched arms waiting for him, voices croaking, "Blood. Blood. Blood. Blood," their long dead throats full of dust and dirt, barely able to make an audible sound. He couldn't stop; he had to push through, had to keep moving for he knew as soon as he stopped one would surely bite him. The temptation was too great. He knew that they couldn't help it. They were human beings, once anyway, but no one can resist hunger forever. Bel remembered his father's dog and the tricks they would play on him. His father loved to put a treat right on the dog's nose, sometimes even on top of his head. The dog wasn't allowed to eat the treat until his father said so. It seemed to little Bel like such a mean thing to do but still it amazed him how his father could have such command over the dog. These dead were not dogs; they were not blindly obedient animals. Yet they hungered like our dog never did. When Pa told our dog to not eat the treat, the dog's belly was already full; the treat was only a sweet ending to a meal. These dead are starving; I must keep moving. It was like passing a delicious sandwich inches from the mouth of a starving person—and Bel knew he was the sandwich.

Bel glanced back and the mountain seemed far away; there were at least a thousand dead swinging and swaying in a constantly moving surf between him and the mountain now. He felt like he was a different person then, a person who was running toward the breach but didn't really want to, a person doing it out of duty. Now he no longer wanted to go back; it was pulling him so hard; every fiber of his being was being drawn toward the breach and all he could think about was how to get there faster. He was suddenly like a puppet in a marionette show and in the audience at the same time. Every cell in his brain told Bel that he should be anywhere but here and do everything in his power to get far, far away from this place, yet here he was, sucked towards it like an insect to blue light. Bel squeezed his mage-wood staff tighter and pressed on. Up ahead there was a clearing and there, right there, a bluish glint. It is the light of my master's staff!

Dread dripped off of Bel in his sweat. It invaded his nostrils. It was the nausea in his belly. It was the taste on his tongue. He swished chalky saliva around in his mouth and spit but the foul taste would not go away. He wouldn't have been surprised if his tongue were black. It tasted horrible, dreadful, terrible. But he couldn't keep away; it was drawing him in, pulling him in, calling him to come closer and deeper into a monstrous place full of fetid, rotten dead things and he could not get there fast enough. If the path were clear of dead he would be running towards the breach in a full gallop; it was just so obvious that he needed to get there as soon as he could but still, he couldn't understand why.

He pushed through another group of dead but tripped on a leg and nearly fell. There were just too many of them. He waved his staff above his head and pushed a small amount of love into the mage-wood, not a lot, just a little, just enough. He didn't want to create a stampede. He didn't want a few thousand confused and disoriented dead full of panic and fear running and trampling him or his master and the others. A pinkish purplish puff surrounded him and the ghoul-kind quickly leapt back, smashing into each other, some tumbling, trying to escape the cloud of Fear. Bel plodded it out of his staff and in front of him, clearing a path through the dead as he slowly stepped through.

"Master? Master? I am coming! I'll be right there!" Bel yelled out to where he last saw the glint of mage-light but he could not see his master or Alexius or Kerlith. He pressed on through the throng to where he last saw the light, hoping that he would find them soon. He was getting close to the breach and did not know what to do. All he knew was that something strong had a hand on his chest and was pulling, drawing him, tugging on him to come closer to the entrance and whatever it was he knew it wanted to kill him.

The sound was getting louder too. It was the roar. The terrible wail that invaded his mind in what seemed like so long ago when they hid out in an abandoned home in the forest. A lifetime ago. I overcame the roar then. Or maybe it just gave up? Bel couldn't be certain of why it left him then but it was certainly here now. And getting louder. It was in his mind and it felt so odd to Bel because around him, for the most part, the ghouls were silent. They stumbled around and he could hear the shuffling of their feet. When he came close to them some would mumble through dry and dusty throats in an almost inaudible croak, but Bel was completely astonished at how quiet several thousand, if not tens of thousands, of wandering corpses could be. But the roar in his mind, that was another story. He wished he could block it out, but it only became louder and stronger the closer he came to the breach.

Bel reached the small clearing and called out again, "Master? Kerlith? Alexius?"

Then something grabbed him and spun him around.

The tug on his shoulder nearly caused him to fall. He jammed his staff into the ground for support, looked down and saw that he was gone. His body was gone. He looked at his staff and where it should have been and then at his missing arms and down at where his legs were supposed to be and they were all gone.

"Nooooooo! The breach has me!" Bel wailed.

"Shhhh! Shut up, Fifth Year! Do you want to get us all killed!" the voice of Nes'egrinon spoke.

Bel looked around and seeing nothing whispered, "Master? Where are you? Are we in the land of the dead? Did we fall into the breach?"

Kerlith's voice said, "We're invisible, stupid."

Nes'egrinon said, "Snuff out your mage-light and grab Alexius' shoulder. Keep your eyes peeled. We're trying to find someone or something that would give us an indication as to what is keeping this rift open."

Bel reached out in the air with his hands and swung them softly, trying to hit a body part, trying to find Alexius, still not understanding what had happened to him.

"That's me," Kerlith said. "Here give me your hand." Kerlith traced Bel's hand back to Alexius' shoulder.

"Okay. I'm ready."

The invisible band stepped slowly, centipede-like towards the breach in a circuitous pattern giving them ample time to cast their amazed eyes at the giant tear in the fabric of reality glistening and pulsing in front of them. It was a large black jagged hole, very tall but not very wide. They could see nothing past it's opening yet corpses would occasionally pop out of the blackness or drop into it as if they were crossing the threshold of a doorway, instantly appearing or disappearing. Bel so desperately wanted to know how this was possible and the tug on his chest so desperately wanted him to cross the threshold but he dared not.

"Ela. Ela. Ela. Ela."

"Did… did any of you hear that?" Bel questioned nervously.

No one responded.

"Ela. Ela. Ela. Ela," sang in Bel's mind again, the mage-words, commanding him to come, the words that he often used to call the light, to call the light to join with his inner light, but now it was death calling to the death within him. It was darkness calling to darkness to join. And he felt the pull and he didn't like what that meant. Every First Year knew that you must have light within you to call to light. But if darkness is calling to me, what does that mean? I can feel the pull. Does that mean that I have death inside me?

Bel's skin began to crawl. He didn't like being invisible. He didn't like that the dead were visible while he was not. He didn't like the fact that something dark, deep within the underworld, was pulling on him to merge with it. The fact that he just killed a man by draining his life-force, albeit unintentionally, dragged on his mind. He felt filthy, dirty and rotten. He was a killer, a murderer, and he deserved to be there in the land of the dead; he deserved to join with the darkness. Maybe he did have death inside him.

Kerlith's voice shook, "I can't. I can't do this. Please. Please, stop me. I can barely control myself."

"What? What are you talking about, boy?" Nes'egrinon spat.

"The darkness calls me! I can barely control it. It wants me to run into the breach."

Nes'egrinon blindly grabbed Kerlith's arm and held it tight. "You have to keep it together, Apprentice. For your master. Do this for your master! Keep it together! Or all is lost!"

"Ela. Ela. Ela. Ela." They all heard it again.

Kerlith was nearly in tears, straining against the archmage's pull. "The life I pulled out of the one-armed boy. It was tainted. Infected. I shouldn't have! The blackness is inside of me! It is being drawn into the breach. I feel I must go."

"I feel it too. You must fight it!" the wizard barked.

Kerlith released his hand from the old man's shoulder and wrestled away from his grasp then began walking toward the breach. He became visible. They all did.

Nes'egrinon slammed his staff into the ground and

screamed in a panic, "Apocalypse!"

The ground trembled and an orb of light erupted from the tip of his staff and swallowed everyone then quickly dissipated. Kerlith continued to walk toward the gaping hole. Alexius ran forward and placed a hand on Kerlith's arm but Kerlith flung it back, sending Alexius into the air. The soldier landed crumpled on the ground and struggled to get up. Kerlith screamed, "Don't touch me! Don't try to stop me!"

Nes'egrinon was hunched over, gasping. With great difficulty he arched his back and raised his arms high and slammed the staff into the ground in front of him. "Apocalypse!" Again the light flashed out, ripples careening across the valley, then was gone.

Bel was unfamiliar with that particular word and thought perhaps that his master was trying to destroy the breach before Kerlith fell into it. Didn't apocalypse mean 'destruction'? Wasn't it the word used to describe the end of the world? He didn't know what his master was doing but he wanted to buy him more time. Bel welled up power into his belly, concentrating it, focusing it, then sent a pulse out his arms and through his pointed staff. The ball of energy careened into Kerlith's legs knocking him to the earth, him stumbling, tumbling, like a child's plaything tossed out of a toy box.

Kerlith leapt to his feet and howled, "You! That's it! I've had enough of you! This ends now!" He ripped out the stone that was hanging from his neck, breaking the thin rope necklace and pointed both fists at Bel, the neck stone in one hand and the stone ring on the other, both glowing brightly. Kerlith's lip quivered feverishly and Bel knew from the contorted painful look on his face that the darkness had his former classmate's mind.

Nes'egrinon heaved his staff once more. "Apocalypse!"

Bel prepared himself. He would fight Kerlith. Now or later, it made no difference. But at least now he was doing it to save his life. He would try not to kill him in doing so. "You want some of this! I'm here!"

Alexius quickly scrambled out of their way.

The old wizard desperately swung his stick of mage-wood and screamed out the words of the old language again, pushing out his energy, draining what little he had. This time as the light washed out and softly faded, a trace of a man standing in the center of the breach appeared. It was then that Bel remembered that the mage-word apocalypse meant "revelation." His master was calling for what was hidden to be revealed, for darkness to show itself.

The ghoul stepped out from the breach, stood in front of them and laughed hysterically, "Hahahahahaha." He took a swig of blood and said, "Enough of this entertainment. You will be of no use to me if you fight and waste all of your energy on each other."

Kerlith's face softened then he looked down at his

feet. Bel snuffed the light out of his staff and walked up to his classmate. Kerlith looked up at him, confused and distraught. Knowing what he was feeling, Bel said, "It's okay," then walked back behind his master. Kerlith shook his head briskly and joined him.

Nes'egrinon braced himself on his staff and Alexius grabbed his arm to prop him up. "Rylith, what have you done?"

"Ah old friend, even now you refuse to acknowledge me? Cutting the honor from my name? Well then, I will call you by the name of your youth also. Nestor. A long time since anyone has called you that, eh? By the way did you see your son on the path? Hahaha."

The wizard replied, "I did. I gave him a spanking. Fleck. I called him Fleck. You know that."

"Ah, I do. You tricked us all. But now I've met him and he has told me your secret."

"Rylith, we have known each other for many years, more years than I care to count. Please tell me you are not responsible for this."

"And two apprentices you have, I see? How does that feel? You know, lads, your master here has only ever had two apprentices, both dead of course. And now he has two at the same time! What are you planning to do? Kill them both together?"

"We must stop this, Rylith. Please, we must. Do you not see what is before you? The dead walk among the living."

Rylithnon refused to acknowledge the old man but continued to address Bel and Kerlith, "Listen, young apprentices. It was not long since you left my charge at Lasaat. Many things I would have you know when you were at the University but it was not convenient to say them there. But now, here, there is no need for secrets. Tell me this, do you know how your master received that nice scar on his face? Perhaps you have figured it out already, no?"

Bel and Kerlith looked at each other, their hands still clenching their weapons. Neither spoke.

"Well I'll tell you. The great and honorable mage before you tried to use the mage-words of the creature-kind. Think of it! A woodland magician! Using the language of... Which was it anyway, Nestor? You never told me? Felis? It was, wasn't it? Oh my! Cats! The language of the feline-kind! I had hoped so! Which dialect? From Percia? Or Otomani?"

"Rylith, this is insane! What are you doing? We must stop this! We must close this hole!"

Anger flashed into the dead mage's voice. "Why? So I can be trapped there? With the dead in the darkness? I don't think so! I quite like it here among the living and I plan to stay here. Sure, I made a mistake. It got away from me and... I died. I think. Yeah, I think I died." The wizard looked down and shook his head slowly then took another draft from his cup of blood. "I died, didn't I? Well, no matter. I'm here now and I am not helping you to close this gateway. Hahahaha. Even if I knew how, I wouldn't. I'm not going back there. Not to stay anyway."

Nes'egrinon motioned for Bel and Kerlith to give him more space. He continued talking to the dead mage while they slowly stepped back. "But you did do this right? You did cause this… this thing here, didn't you?"

The dead mage replied, "Probably."

"How?"

"I guess I can tell you. You can't stop me anyway. I'm already dead! Hahahaha." Rylithnon smiled then continued proudly, "Well, the moon was full. I was here, in my lands, the stone lands, in the valley of the dead; my magic would be strongest here. I should have been able to control it. Yes! I should have. Just a small spell, a little forest magic. Then a small casting from the words of the tundra. It was working! It did feel a bit odd though. Peculiar. I don't know why it felt so, but it worked! I know what you are thinking. Heresy. That is why I had to do it out here. The others would never understand. And with Sturfelis' infernal eyes everywhere I had to get somewhere where there was nothing that he could see through. No animals, no birds, no trees, just cold hard rock. It had to be here."

Alexius interrupted, "But this? How could your magic lead to this?"

The dead man drank again and replied, "I don't know. But I'll figure it out. Next time I'll control it. Dead or no I'll unite all magic. I'll cast the one spell. I'll find it, the one spell that works in all lands and among all creature-kind, the words spoken at the beginning of creation, the words of unification."

Bel could stand no more. "Again! You are going to do it again! Look what you did the first time! How much worse do you plan on making this? You'll destroy the planet!"

"Destroy? I will create! Don't you see! You of all should know! Why do you think I kept you back? You tasted it; you should know! Ha! And not even yet an apprentice. Do you know that you, of all people, gave me the courage to do this? I have you to thank! I'd studied for far too long. For too long I'd been afraid to step out and just do it. It took a young boy, barely past his Third Year's training—you may as well been still in diapers! It took you, doing what you did, to convince me to step out and do this. It's fitting that you are here now, that you would be one of the few here to witness what I am about to do."

Nes'egrinon blew on the tip of his staff and it suddenly burst into flame. "I cannot allow you to do that."

Rylithnon paused, furrowed his brow, and then replied, "I'm sorry to hear that. If you try to stop me then you will die."

Chapter Seventeen

Rylithnon

Nes'egrinon whispered, "Alexius, Kerlith, Fifth Year, I need you to stay well back. Don't get in the way. Keep my back safe. Don't let the ghouls sweep in from behind me. I don't yet know if he controls them."

Bel thought, Maybe that is why we pushed through them so easily? Rylithnon wanted us here?

Alexius nodded, withdrew his sword and walked back about ten paces as Kerlith and Bel pushed love out into small puffs of purple and pink haze, frightening the surrounding ghoul-kind, clearing a small circle around the entrance to the breach. Nes'egrinon stood in the center of the circle, an old, broken looking man, forcing himself to stand upright when it was clear that his back wished to stoop low and crooked, his gnarled, oversized knuckles twisted around a worn out stick.

Rylithnon, still standing at the breach entrance, faced him with a broad smile. They had been friends—they both said as much—friends that disagreed often yet knew each other well enough to voice those disagreements and still work together afterwards. Yet Rylithnon smiled at this upcoming duel for some odd reason.

His mind cannot be right, Bel thought. The glint in his eye and the peculiar way his cheek twitches? No, he's just not right. He's gone soft in the head.

The dead wizard guzzled blood, drinking much more than the last time, and then pointed his arms at the ground, his fingers extended and rolling. The ground began to shimmer. "You cannot win, you know! Look around you! Look where you are, mage of the forest!"

Stones trembled in place violently. The dead stumble-stepped further away. Some ran toward the mountain.

The two apprentices and Alexius tried to find somewhere to brace themselves. Alexius ran awkwardly over to a boulder and placed his hands on it trying to steady himself but the boulder was shaking briskly too. Bel went down to one knee and placed his hands on the ground. Nausea crept into his stomach. All the while, Nes'egrinon slowly twisted his staff in the ground.

A small rock popped into the air and Rylithnon waived his hand sending it flying. In the blackness, Nes'egrinon did not see it coming. The rock smacked him on the cheek, splitting it open.

"Now do you see my power? Now do you see why you cannot stop me? While you have sat idle in your precious wood for the last half millennia, I have been studying, perfecting my craft, learning the words and their meanings and usages, developing a metaphysical connection to the language. You speak words. But I, much more. I use sentences!"

"Rylith, you know I've had just about enough of your bravado for one lifetime! You never stop talking about all that you can do. Don't you know no one cares about your boasts?"

The dead wizard flicked his wrist and another stone flew toward Nes'egrinon. "And you? Why should I listen to you? What have you done? Oh, your name is out there for some past deeds. I'll give you that one. A bard or two has immortalized you because you were in the right place at the right time. I haven't been as lucky but all will know my name now."

"If a name is all you want then I will spread it myself. I will speak of your great accomplishments. Just, please, let go of this insanity. Help me to close this rift and I'll tell everyone that the great Rylithnon did it. You're the best. Really you are."

Rylithnon waived his hand again and several sharp pebbles flew at the old wizard. He covered his face with his arm this time but one still struck his neck, cutting him.

The dead wizard screamed back, "Insanity? Insanity? What's insane is sitting idly by and watching the world pass before your eyes. I'm tired of talking about accomplishments. You think I care about what everyone thinks? I don't care what *anyone* thinks! What did we teach in the University? Seize the day? Embrace life and live it? Now feel my embrace!"

The dead magician placed his hand on the ground and grimaced as if he was severely constipated. A few moments later a large boulder, taller than a man, rolled down the mountain toward them. "Now you'll see!" Rylithnon said.

Corpses fled from the huge rock's path, it accelerating as it continued toward the breach.

"Here it comes! You're about to taste my power!"

The boulder bounced as it struck rocks on the ground, shattering them into rubble.

"Any moment now. You'll see. That big boulder is coming."

Bel and Kerlith turned their heads to look at the approaching boulder, then back at Rylithnon, then back over to the boulder. Nes'egrinon stared intently at the dead wizard, refusing to look back. Bel and Kerlith stared at the rock and then toward Rylithnon.

"It'll be the end of you. You'll see. You'll see. It's coming to smash you. Any moment now."

As the huge hunk rolled into the circle, the old wizard

swung his staff behind his head, its tip striking the approaching stone behind him, splitting it into two, its forward motion arrested and the two broken halves falling to either side.

Rylithnon shook his hands in the air, visibly upset. "See? I worked on that spell for weeks and you didn't even look back at it to see your impending doom. How disrespectful!"

"Doom? It's you who are doomed."

"Enough goofing around!" Rylithnon extended his hands and rolled his fingers, each having a large stone ring on it, the rings slowly glowing brighter and brighter. Streams of ghoul-kind emerged from the blackness of the breach behind Rylithnon, appearing to pop into existence, some in the full battle dress of the great Achaean warrior and others wearing all manner of foreign dress: large men with reddish hair and wearing patterned clothing carrying large hammers or balls hanging from the ends of chains; naked warriors carrying wooden spears; short, squarish, yellow-skinned men with long black hair and curved swords; and hairy faced giants wearing thick, furry clothing with double-sided axes in hand. They poured in and formed a wall alongside of the dead wizard, all of them moaning, groaning and croaking, their vacant, dead eyes staring forward.

"Shall I introduce you to my new friends?" Rylithnon turned his head toward them and pointed his outstretched arm at Nes'egrinon. "See, my friends. I told you. Look upon this old man. He's all that stands between you and freedom from your prison. Destroy him and I can set you free."

"Lies!" Nes'egrinon yelped. "He lies to you!"

Some of the group started forward but then stopped when the old wizard began to speak. Nes'egrinon continued, "Achaeans, brothers, some of you must remember me and the wisdom of my council. Surely you know I would not be here for ill."

One stepped forward and said, "This is my old friend, Nestor, who stands before us. How long has it been that you still walk with the living? You were old when we stood side by side at the siege of Ilium. No. We cannot stand against him. He is one of us."

Several of them turned to the blackness and popped out of sight, disappearing without a perceptible sign of retreat. One moment they were there; the next they were not as if the breach had somehow breathed them back in.

"No, no, no. No!" Rylithnon yelled.

A large giant of a man with an axe in his hand, his body covered with the skin of a bear, said, "This man I do not know. And if I did, I probably wouldn't care anyway. The wizard says we must kill him to be free from this place. That I will do easy enough. If the wizard lies to us then I will remove his head. Sounds like fun, either way."

The group agreed and charged, several of the naked

warriors throwing their spears in the air ahead of them, screaming, "Aaaaaaaahhhhh!" Others swung their chains and metal balls. The men with curved swords held them to the side pointed straight, running fast. Alexius readied himself, both hands on the hilt of his sword. Bel and Kerlith swung their tools, stone and staff, grabbing individuals near the ends with their magic and heaving them into the air, flinging them far off onto the mountain. Nes'egrinon spun in a circle, dragging his staff on the ground, mumbling words of the old language. Soon a circle of blue light surrounded them. The dead warriors stopped instinctively at the border of light.

The spears sailed through the air but the four easily dodged them as their points buried in the earth with a thud.

"What are you doing? Why are you stopping?" Rylithnon screamed, spittle flying off of his dead lips. "Oh. A spell of protection from the dead. I forgot about that one." He lifted his hands high and a large boulder rose in the air. It coasted through the ether toward the old wizard.

"Kerlith! Do something!" Bel yelled.

"I… I don't know what to—"

"Something! Do something!"

Kerlith stepped forward, pushed both arms out into the air as if he would catch the giant stone coming at them, his head pointed down, eyes squeezed shut. The boulder pierced the barrier and the warrior-ghouls cheered. The flying rock reached Kerlith and slowed as it reached his hands as if the air around it had thickened. It landed upon him and he screamed as his legs slowly buried into the ground, deeper and deeper into the ground. His arms began to bend unnaturally under the intense weight. Bel got behind him and put his hands on Kerlith's back, pushing his energy into him, the boulder grinding against Bel's face as Kerlith sunk lower into the earth.

"Push! Push, Kerlith!"

Kerlith screamed as he both drew energy from Bel and pushed on the giant rock. The boulder turned a little, then a little more as Kerlith gained control of it. It rolled to the side, landed on the ground and continued to roll. Bel helped a panting Kerlith to free his legs from the earth and Nes'egrinon walked toward the large stone and tapped it with his stick. The boulder continued to roll then picked up speed, rolling toward the warriors. In a panic they leapt out of the way. The boulder sailed into the breach and disappeared.

Rylithnon chuckled, "So, the great defender of what is normal and right, the mage of the wood uses stone magic once again?"

"My hand never left my staff," replied Nes'egrinon in a growl.

"I see. I see. Hahahaha." The dead wizard looked

hysterical, one moment laughing uncontrollably then the next pensive. "Maybe that is what I have been missing? You are a wood mage so your hands never leave your staff of mage-wood, yet you control the stone. I, a stone mage, must do likewise; I must need to channel my magic through stones?"

Bel finally pulled Kerlith from the ground but Kerlith's feet, legs and ankles were severely gashed and bleeding.

Nes'egrinon barked at the dead wizard, "What you need to do is either help close this breach or step out of the way and let me do it." The old wizard was visibly exhausted. Bel hoped his master had an idea of how to close the rift.

"Help? You?" Rylithnon gulped more blood then laughed again. He pointed his left arm at the sky and his right at the wizard then opened his mouth wide. He looked wild-eyed and hungry, as if with his mouth open he could somehow swallow all men, all birds, all beasts and all life, rapaciously, ravenously, as if he could suck away all the air and swallow the very earth in one voracious bite. A deep guttural sound emerged and slowly reached Bel and the band, reverberating through them. A dark swirling cloud appeared above Rylithnon. No one would have been able to detect it in the black sky except that in the cloud were all manner of lightning. Thunder roared. In the utter darkness of the valley the bolts of light were such a shock that even though the living sheltered their eyes they were momentarily blinded. Many of the dead ran for fear.

A strong gale force blew and they fought to not be blown from their feet. Rylithnon tried to speak, tried to taunt them again but the wind was deafening. They couldn't hear a word he said. The naked men with spears, the dead warriors from a long past day ran back to the breach and disappeared. Rylithnon screamed at them, apparently cursing their cowardice, but no one could hear his words.

Nes'egrinon pointed for the others to get far behind him as he held his staff in front of him. Just as the three got behind a few large boulders and an outcropping of dirt, a bolt of electricity streamed down through the sky, erupting from the large cloud, lighting up the sky and striking Rylithnon's outstretched arm. The dead wizard shone bright white; the voltage permeated his body and then extended out from his arm that was pointed at Nes'egrinon all the while. Large flakes of skin popped off Rylithnon's face and arms as the energy flowed through him and out his arm toward the mage of the forest. Light burst from the flesh underneath. The bolt struck Nes'egrinon's outstretched staff, it glowing blue as the energy filled it then slowly crept into the wizard's hand then his arm then his body. He gasped loudly, "Aaaaahhhh!" but no one could hear it for the resounding boom of the electricity was ear splitting.

There was a final flash of light then utter darkness. No one could see for the impulse had blinded them all. They sat silent and waiting as their eyes adjusted. Bel only hoped that his eyes would adjust before the ghoul-kind. He blinked and squinted then blinked and squinted and finally he could barely make out his hand just inches from his face, but it was enough. He stood and peered over the boulder to see a fuzzy image. He tried to piece together what he was seeing. It appeared to be his master, lying on the earth, wisps of steam emanating from his body, his clothing singed and burnt and Rylithnon standing over him. But that couldn't be right. Bel stood and walked toward them, not able to make mental sense of the images that his eyes were showing him.

"Come! Come! Come and see, young Bel!" Rylithnon said as he motioned with his hand. "See? See? I have you to thank for this! Look! The great Nes'egrinon, defeated and lying at my feet." Rylithnon's skin was mostly torn from his face revealing sinewy muscle and tendon and cartilage and the fullness of his eyes sockets. None of the exposed muscle was red or even light pink like Bel thought it would have been; it was the gray of long over-boiled meat. He looked monstrous. And he smelled none too nice.

Bel's voice shook. "You don't have me to thank. I had no part in this."

The wizard noticed another piece of flesh hanging from his hand so he shook it off. "As you wish. But still you are here and your eyes will see it. My glory. My ascension." The dead wizard stretched out his arms and began to slowly float up. He tilted back his head to the sky and twelve stones, each about the size of a man's head, formed a circle around him from head to foot. The stones began to rotate.

Bel ignored the dead wizard's gloating and slowly walked back to his position behind the boulders to gather with Alexius and Kerlith. "We have to do something."

"Aye. But what can we three do against one such as this?" Alexius replied.

Kerlith mumbled, "We have to do something. We have to try."

The spell of protection began to fade and the three knew that Nes'egrinon was unconscious. Or dead.

The three stood as the stones continued to circle the elevated wizard, lightning alternately striking a stone or two. Bel thought, This must be how he did it before. This must be it, the spell that ripped open the breach, the spell he cast to unite all magic, the one spell. He's going to try it again and we are all going to die.

They walked to below where he floated. The remaining warriors screamed when they saw them there and charged them. Alexius parried, blocked, swung his sword and spun, fighting against several of the red haired warriors with broad chests and long boots, wearing the traditional green plaid of the highlands.

Bel screamed, "Apokrothos!" sending one dead warrior after another flying off into the sky, landing several hundred paces away, some flying further, off onto the mountain. Kerlith pushed the purple haze of love magic at fur covered warrior after warrior sending them screaming in fear but he was getting weaker. They all were. He would have loved to send out on large puff of love, like they had done previously, but that would take just too much energy and they had so little to spare.

Bel and Kerlith ran to Alexius' aid after they dispatched the dead they were fighting. Bel pushed life-force into his staff and used it as a club to smack a highlander back into the breach. Kerlith sent stones flying, pelting the warriors until they ran.

After the dead warriors were gone Alexius rubbed a gash on his forearm and said, "I am sorry that I am not of much use to you two."

Bel and Kerlith ignored the comment and looked down at Nes'egrinon's smoldering body. They looked at each other with a mixture of defeat and resignation in their eyes, as if their fate was a foregone conclusion. Bel said, "Can you do anything?"

Kerlith replied, "I doubt it. But I must try."

"Then we will do it together." Bel stood next to Kerlith and grabbed his hand, them both facing the floating Rylithnon.

Alexius stood behind them. "I cannot do much to help you but I will give you my energy. My... my life-force, I will give it to you. Just do what you can." He placed his hands on the two boys' backs and looked down at the ground, squeezing his eyes shut hard. Bel knew what it meant. He knew he had drained Kephas earlier and he bristled at the idea of draining Alexius but he didn't argue. He accepted the gift. They would all be dead soon anyway.

Kerlith began chanting words in the stone language, the old words only known by the stone-mages of the east, passed down century after century from master to apprentice in an oral tradition that went back to the dawn of time itself. Bel had no idea what he was saying so he began speaking words in the forest language, trying to disrupt the rotation of stone after rapidly circling stone, trying to shift them out of orbit, to somehow weaken Rylithnon's spell or at least distract him from what he was doing so that Kerlith might have more of a chance. He sent out a breeze, a spell of forest magic, wind from the trees. A stone wobbled. Then another. But each time they immediately swung back on track. Sometimes even accelerating. Rylithnon ignored them as if they weren't even there. Bel wanted to send a stiff breeze, even a gust to knock the dead mage back but he knew something like that would take too much energy. It would kill Alexius and what would it accomplish?

Kerlith huffed, "Keep the wind up."

Bel's ears perked up and he pushed out another blast.

One rock swung a little off course and Kerlith grunted as he squeezed onyx. A rock from the ground flew up and hit the off course stone cracking it in half. One half flew away while the other crashed into Rylithnon.

The dead mage squealed, "You! I didn't slay you so that you might witness my work. I gave you a space to breathe because of what you did at Lasaat and how you helped to open my eyes but now you will die." The floating wizard raised his arms high, the muscle fibers on his skinless arms exposed as his sleeves slid down.

The three braced themselves but before he could send out the spell a bolt of electricity smote him, striking his chest. The three turned to see Nes'egrinon trying to stand up, using his staff for leverage.

"Master! You're not dead!" Bel ran to his side quickly then slowed. "Are you dead?"

Alexius and Kerlith joined him.

"No time for talk! We must hit him now! With everything!" Nes'egrinon bellowed.

The two young men quickly spun and pushed out magic toward Rylithnon who was still floating awkwardly in the air. Nes'egrinon swung his staff, causing lightning to strike the dead wizard again and again.

Nes'egrinon screamed, "Fight it! Fight it! Push out all

of the darkness! Shine forth your light!"

Rylithnon covered his face in the crook of his elbow as he was smashed back again and again from several different directions.

Bel screamed, "I can feel it leaving now! The darkness. It leaves me!" It pushed out another blast of energy. He didn't know how much more he had but as long as he could, he would fight the darkness. He knew now more than ever that the darkness' biggest weapon was to make him feel like he couldn't win, to try to make him give up.

Rylithnon floated toward the breach entrance and realizing where he was yelled, "No!"

Kerlith sent a stone careening at Rylithnon who swam in the air to dodge it. Bel blasted him with a gust of air and Nes'egrinon with lightning.

Nes'egrinon and Bel looked at each other momentarily somehow knowing what they each were thinking without a word or a nod. They both yelled, "Phos! Phos! Phos! PHOS!" and a blinding mage-light erupted in front of them casting vibrant blue, illuminating the entire valley, even piercing the very breach itself.

Rylithnon popped out of existence, falling into the dark tear. And suddenly it was gone. The breach was gone.

Bel mumbled in disbelief, "The breach? It's gone?" Then louder, "The breach is gone." He looked around and did not see anything moving, no person, no ghoul, not anything living or dead but only dirt and rock met his eyes outside of the band of four lonely wanderers. Then, just past the eastern mountains, a glimmer of light appeared as the sun eased above the far ridge. It was the dawn of a new day.

Nes'egrinon hugged Bel then roped in Kerlith and Alexius. Bel laughed and cried and screamed, "The breach is gone!"

Chapter Eighteen

Truth Shines

Bel sat and watched them as the light of the noonday sun shone brightly.

A woman gathered her rough, variegated burlap and felt clothing into a large basket, preparing to wash while two small freckled children chased each other around her knees. A man stepped out of the front door of a dilapidated shack and scratched himself. Across the street an old man with splotchy, mottled skin rocked back and forth on the rear legs of a chair, one hand on a long pipe, puffing on it slowly.

Bel looked at the children, then the woman, then the man, then finally the old man rocking.

Fluttering finch wings grabbed his attention as the tiny birds swung round, too fickle to find a place to land.

The faint but distinct trap clap, trap clap, trap clap of approaching horses alerted everyone that visitors were coming and soon enough three men rode up from the path and secured their horses. They brushed the dust and grime off their thick red and green jackets and pants then entered the inn. Bel knew what called them as he could also smell it, the salty fresh scent of malt wafting throughout the town as the barkeeper's son stirred the bitters behind the inn. The two children ran over to get a closer look at the horses. Across the way a middle-aged woman set out a pie on the sill and cinnamon scent curled under Bel's nose trying to lure him like a fisherman's hook.

Bel couldn't help but marvel. It was but a few short days ago that the world was ending and there were ghoul-kind everywhere devouring flesh. Now all was as if it never happened. The resiliency of human-kind was mind boggling to Bel. There was day. There was night. And the only creatures that walked the earth were living. All was as it should be.

"Tell me what you see," Nes'egrinon said.

The question shook Bel's mind from its wandering. "What do you mean?"

"Just what I said. Tell me what you see."

"I see nothing special. What I don't see are ghouls. That's good. They're gone. No more ghouls. No more dead walking among the living."

Nes'egrinon moved to stand next to Bel. "I didn't ask

you to tell me what you don't see. I asked you to tell me what you see."

"Nothing special. I don't know what you are looking for." Bel paused and looked up at the old man.

The wizard looked down and squinted his dissatisfaction.

Bel looked back out at the small village center and continued, "I see an old man leaning on the edge of his chair. He's smoking something. A small family here. They are attending to routine things. I see children playing. A mother readying her clothing to wash. There's an inn there and people are going in and out, travelers and such. Not much. Just everyday life. Normal stuff."

"Exactly." Nes'egrinon smiled as he took a seat next to the boy.

"I don't understand."

"What you are seeing. You said it. What you are seeing is life. Life. These people are living it. Just everyday life. Don't you get it?"

"No," Bel replied as he shook his head slowly.

"The source of all our power, of all power everywhere, the very act of creation from the very beginning is life."

"All First Years are taught that."

The old man spoke softly, "But did you learn? Look and see. Open your eyes. The power that we ask to work for us is life itself. It is in every living being and every creature and here it is right in front of you; life being lived. This is the only true source of magic."

The two were silent for a time, Bel thoughtful and observant, Nes'egrinon smiling widely.

"Master, how did we do it? How did we defeat Rylithnon? Why did the breach slam closed?"

"It is hard to say. Darkness always flees from light, does it not?"

"I suppose," Bel replied somewhat unsatisfied. "But was it our magic?"

"Now that is an insightful question. I like to think that it wasn't. I like to think that it was something inside of us. That somehow, when we rejected the pull, when we rejected the darkness inside of ourselves that we somehow caused something to happen. That the act of resistance, of fighting against the darkness, was enough to defeat it. In my experience evil is always defeated if we stand, face it and fight it. It is only when we give up that we lose to the darkness."

"Maybe. Yes. I think that is true." Bel paused as he watched the children. "I'm just sure glad that you weren't dead."

"Me too. It is amazing that we made it through. Kerlith and Alexius too; I was glad to return them to the Keep. What other questions do you have that I cannot answer?" Nes'egrinon beamed. He was in an uncharacteristically delightful mood.

"I have many questions. I am sure you can answer

some. Others probably not. What is to become of Kerlith, I wonder. Will he find a new master? Since you are not a seer, I'm sure you will not know. How did you call the great birds that carried us out of the stone lands and back to the Keep? Now that is a question I really would like answered but perhaps you will say that I'm not ready to know. I'd love to know about your son, how did you have him and how did he become your apprentice? I'd love to know all of that but of course it would be inappropriate for me to ask. Maybe one day I'll find out. Yes, I have many questions. But for now I would be content to relax and watch these people live life in the full light of the noonday sun."

The two looked back out at the people as they went about doing things. After a time Nes'egrinon said with a wide smile, "Apprentice," as he placed his arm around Bel's neck and rested his old wrinkled hand on his shoulder. "Tomorrow we start your training. Tomorrow you start your journey. Never again will I call you Fifth Year for at this moment you have become my apprentice."

Reviews Please!

If you have enjoyed this book, please be so kind as to provide a review of it on both goodreads and the online shopping site you most frequent. This will serve the dual purpose of letting me know what you thought of it which will influence my future writing and also help expose the book to other potential readers. Thank you so much.

Follow Me For Deals!

I occasionally put my books on sale or discount. If you would like to keep track of my writing and when new books are coming out, when they're on sale and other such things, please follow or friend me on goodreads. Additionally, join my mailing list from my website at www.jamescardona.com.

Feedback!

If you would like to give either of us direct personal feedback, you can message us on goodreads.

Acknowledgements

The authors would like to thank a handful of readers and fellow authors who have taken the time to carefully review this book and provide meaningful feedback to make it that much better.

Emily Beckwith

Tracy Boehmer

Terri Christie

Kirsten Jany

Marc Secchia

247

Coming Soon

The Dragon's Castle

The Apprentice Series 2

ISBN 978-1-5059-1626-3

A young adult action packed fantasy romance adventure that will keep readers guessing as mystery after mystery unfolds. Bel, a wizard's apprentice accompanies his master to the capitol city to help negotiate a truce between warring kingdoms, but when they arrive he finds much more than he bargained for. His long lost love, Shireen is there and their romance is quickly rekindled. There's only one problem with that though-magician's are to remain celibate under penalty of excommunication.

It's a fantasy tale that sizzles, sparkles and pops with energy, ingenuity, imagination, and a wonderfully heightened sense of adventure.

All Bel wants to do is train under his master. He just acquired a full wizard's staff, at great difficulty, so he has no interest in going off on some boring trek to negotiate a truce. But when they arrive, all is not what it seems. He finds that Shireen is apprentice under Meetta and Bel can't keep his eyes off his former love. His master seems to have a strange, hypnotic attraction for Meetta, but that couldn't be right, could it? Wizard's aren't allowed! A fellow wizard, Gedd, from a neighboring kingdom seems to know just a little to much about how and why the kingdoms are at war. Is he influencing them? The avians and the birds they control are everywhere. What do they seek? Readers everywhere are calling it "compelling," "amazing" and a "story that draws you in and sweeps you off your feet."

This young adult, fantasy romance adventure is told from the perspective of Bel, Shireen, Meetta and Nes'egrinon, the two apprentices and their two masters as they each try to figure out what is going on as the kingdoms stagger-step close and closer to war, while trying to sort out their intense feelings for each other.

Bel and Shireen fall in love all over again and it is only after they come to this stark realization that they don't know what to do about it. It is the trade that every wizard must make. To become a magician they must forsake all relationships; they must give up love to gain knowledge. What choice will Bel and Shireen make? Are they strong enough? Can they give each other up? Should they?

Reviewers are saying of this young adult, action packed, fast paced, romantic adventure, "a perfect marriage of fantasy and romance. I was gushing for their love affair and bouncing through the action scenes. I couldn't get enough of it."

Bel learns of the history of the kingdoms and all is not so rosy as there is bad blood of the decades that is coming to call. The avians and the creature-kind have not forgotten their losses at the hands of the Greenland warriors and the Eastern Forest Kingdom is pushing to expand. The forest is full of adversaries, each of which having different motivations and goals. Yet one thing they all have in mind, to conquer the capitol city. That is where the four wizards find themselves, at the center of a besieged city, surrounded by soldiers eager for blood.

It's a fast paced, young adult adventure tale full of swords and sorcery, mythical creatures, animals and dragons. The dragon's castle is sure to delight fans of fantasy romance drama.

Part thriller, part fantasy, and part mystery, The Dragon's Castle is suspenseful and exhilarating to read. It is impossible to put down.

Also by James Cardona

Santa Claus vs. The Aliens

ISBN 978-0-9850284-6-6

Finalist 2014 — Wishing Shelf Children's Book Awards

In this fast paced, Children's holiday science fiction adventure, Edwin, a fourteen year old and an odd character dressed as Santa Claus attempt to stop aliens and save the planet in 1950's Manhattan.

When Edwin cuts his finger, dripping a few drops of blood onto a bone-colored tracking device he becomes a target of a group of aliens that think he holds the secret to the human race's defeat. The only person who seems to know what to do is a fat man wearing a Santa Claus suit and he somehow seems to know just a little too much.

Who is he and why does he know so much? Where did the aliens come from and what are they after? Can a Fourteen year old wandering the cold, empty streets of Manhattan late on Christmas Eve and an odd character dressed as Santa Claus stop the aliens, save the planet and discover the true meaning of Christmas?

Readers are calling it **"packed with humor, action"** and **"adventure"** and **"intelligent and thoroughly enjoyable."** Grab hold of this children's science fiction Christmas adventure and take a wild ride.

One day, Edwin's father, Fundy, witnesses a strange object falling out of the sky. When he realizes a person is in it, he helps the red suited man pull his strange vehicle out of the muck with his horse, Paulo. As Santa flies off, he accidentally drops his ring.

After his encounter with the strange man, Fundy and his wife move to the United States, hoping to find happiness, but instead they eventually get divorced, placing Edwin in a children's home when neither of them could take care of their son. When Edwin is dropped off at the children's home, Fundy gives his son his most prized possession, the Santa's ring.

Several years after his divorce, Fundy has remarried,

has a little girl, acquired a decent job, and wishes for Edwin to come back home. Whether for rage or guilt, Edwin cannot bring himself to do this. He feels as though his home is no longer his own, as if a strange woman is living there. Edwin knows that he will no longer see his father and actual mother together ever again, but it's just not right to him.

Called, "an **absolute gem of a story** aimed at our 8 -10 yr olds," it brings "**a wonderful slant to a timeless classic**" that seems to have always lived around Santa Claus and the gift of Christmas, bringing us closer to that Original Christmas.

As the aliens chase Edwin through the cold, dark streets on Christmas Eve, steadily getting closer and closer, you will run with Edwin as he tries to determine what in the world is going on? Who are those people that are chasing him? Why does Santa seem to know about Edwin being tracked?

Amid the dashing through a city to escape strange people chasing him, our hero discovers things about himself that he has never known and learns just how valuable family really is.

During the fight between Edwin, Santa Claus and the aliens, our hero learns just how much difference loyalty and friendship can make and that family values are the real gifts that Christmas brings.

"There is simply something about the character

Edwin that **I really fell in love with and latched on to**. Perhaps it was his family situation and the decision that he had to make when deciding whether to live with his reconstructed family or stay at a children's home that naturally drew me to him." --Annette Huss

A holiday Christmas tale about a dysfunctional family coming together married to a science fiction adventure involving an alien scouting party prior to a full scale alien invasion, this one is sure to please middle grade students and adults alike. Set in a 1950's Manhattan, the book has a retro feel but the situations and family conflicts are timeless. A brisk, fast paced and entertaining novel that constantly engages the reader with new developments, Santa Claus vs the Aliens is full of tense situations interspersed with fun, laughs and comedy.

Also by James Cardona

Gabriella and The Speed of Life

ISBN 978-1506150727

A young adult action packed romance adventure that will keep readers guessing as mystery after mystery unfolds.

Gabriella, teenage girl tries to discover herself in a futuristic world of genetic modification, extreme sports and new science. Oh, and there just happens to be a dimensional portal too.

This science fiction tale **sizzled and sparkled with energy, ingenuity, imagination, and a wonderfully**

heightened sense of adventure! --B White

Gabriella, a teenage girl who lives a simple life selling shoes in her parents clothing store, has her life turned upside down when two NuGen goons show up at their store. Shortly thereafter, her father is dead, tragically, and she finds out the entire life she had been living is a lie. They must change their name, run and hide, leaving everything behind that very night.

So starts the **whirlwind adventure, a mystery set in a futuristic society**, where affluent folks can have their children modified through genetic upgrades, that readers are calling "Compelling," "so good!" and a "great story that draws you in."

Gabriella discovers that she is a surprisingly good athlete and the only "non-modified" able to compete with genetically modified super-athletes. Did she become this way because of a genetic modification experiment her father conducted? Who killed her father and why? Are they after her? (Hint: They are.)

She's offered a spot on a semi-pro farm team in Philadelphia. It's her and her mother's only escape from the dirt and dung of the shanty towns and favelas of Brazil so she takes it. But that puts her squarely in NuGen's sights.

Kyle and Sebastian are NuGen liaisons to the team. Kyle is gorgeous but can he be trusted?

Reviewers are saying of this young adult, action

packed, fast paced, romantic adventure, "I was completely hooked."

Gabriella meets Smith, a researcher who worked with her father. Her mother is smitten but Gabriella doesn't trust him. What should she do? And why does it seem like he's collecting fingerprints off her glass or stray strands of her hair? Why is he so interested in her DNA?

Due to her new-found notoriety, a physicist presents her the opportunity to be the spokesperson for his new invention, the Dimensional Transport Machine. The machine allows for near instantaneous travel across the planet by entering a portal one side of the planet and exiting on another. In between is a different dimension, but there's nothing there so no worries, right? Or is there.

A tightly packed piece of work that demonstrates that this author knows his way around a story. --Robin Lynn

After entering the portal, Gabriella sees a ghost like creature who looks uncharacteristically like her dead father. Is it him? But why doesn't he behave like her father? Why does his voice sound like that? Why doesn't he hug her and love her, instead of being so distant? Who is the man in the Void?

With NuGen on her heels and her father's ominous warnings, Gabriella is on a quest to find out her true identity and solve the mystery of her dad's murder.

Part thriller, part sci-fi, and part mystery,

Gabriella and Dr. Duggan's Secret Dimensional Transport Machine is suspenseful and exhilarating to read. It picks up speed as it goes along, and is impossible to put down. --Kelly

Full of action, drama, comedy, with a fair sprinkling of romance, this book will appeal to the young adult who is looking for a fast paced, edge-of-your-seat adventure full of mysteries that will keep you guessing.

Who is Gabriella? Is she modified? Is her father really her father? Or was she cooked up in a lab? If Gabriella can completely reinvent herself, casting aside her fictional past, who does she want to be?

Using the machine unleashes a bizarre and entertaining series of events that helps Gabriella discover who she is and who she wants to be.

About The Authors

James Cardona has written seven books as yet including two non-fiction works, three young adult science fiction novels and two fantasy novels. He is planning on writing many, many more, including the release of the third installment of the apprentice series in 2015.

For his fiction, James tries to make his words come alive by pouring his real-life experiences into his characters such that many of the details described in his books actually happened and are told from the perspective of someone who was there. He also enjoys integrating a hard science approach to his science fiction, feeling that all aspects of his story telling, although perhaps not currently possible, could actually happen once our technology evolves.

James enjoys all things that can unleash the creative process including drawing, painting and creative writing and the not-so-typical such as robot design and writing computer code. He loves tinkering with computers, electronics and building robots and is the Lead Engineer for FIRST Robotics Team 316, a High School Robotics team operating out of Salem Community College.

Additionally James helps organize and run the PSEG Nuclear Salem County Math Showcase which he created back in the year 2000, a math competition for students from grades four through eight, typically attended each year by approximately 500-600 students.

James received his Bachelor's degree in Computer Science from the University of Delaware with a minor in Religious Studies. He lives in Southern New Jersey and works as a Senior Test Engineer for the Laboratory and Testing Services group of the Public Service Electric and Gas Company.

In his last year of high school, Issa Cardona is feverishly preparing for college, enrollment testing and campus visits. He plans on majoring in Physics and minoring in Mathematics at Rutgers University. In his nonexistent spare time he loves to read science fiction and fantasy and kills at League of Legends. He is also in charge of the mechanical design sub-team on his High School Robotics team.

He thoroughly enjoyed bringing the characters in this book to life, especially Bel and Kerlith. He feels that no matter the time period, generation or situation, teenagers will always be teenagers and the dramatic change, growth and development of this time of life is a perfect foil for the human condition.

www.ingramcontent.com/pod-product-compliance
Lightning Source LLC
Chambersburg PA
CBHW060406180626
46817CB00007B/2532